Hiding her Heart

Hiding her Heart

CATHRYN BROWN

For permission requests, write to the publisher, addressed "Attention: Permissions Coordinator," at the address below.

Sienna Bay Press

PO Box 158582

Nashville, Tennessee 37215

www.cathrynbrown.com

Cover designed by Najla Qamber Designs

(www.najlaqamberdesigns.com)

Hiding her Heart/Cathryn Brown. - 1st ed.

ISBN: 978-1-945527-67-8

❀ Formatted with Vellum

DEAR READER

Randi has been in this series from the beginning, but always in the background. I liked her so much that I wanted to give her a story of her own.

In *Hiding her Heart*, Randi's still running a motel and selling real estate. She's hardworking, loyal, and a little too used to doing things alone. But lately, she's been dreaming of something more.

I had fun bringing John into her life. He's a writer, a wanderer, and someone who didn't expect to find roots—or romance—in Two Hearts.

But sometimes, home and love are waiting where you least expect to find them. Together, they're a great team.

I hope you enjoy John and Randi's story!

CHAPTER ONE

*R*andi Hollis reached out her hand from her position under the bathroom sink. "Michelle, I need that wrench again. The one I just set down."

Michelle placed the metal tool in her hand. "I feel like a nurse beside the doctor during surgery." She laughed. "Not that this hasn't been fun rushing over here to help before the sun came up, but I have just enough time to go home, shower, and change to get to the restaurant for my shift."

Frustration rushed through Randi. Michelle had been a great friend to come here hours ago, but she had a life of her own. Ever since Randi's brother had gotten a job—a great one he couldn't turn down in Phoenix, Arizona—and had signed over his share of the motel to her, she'd been on her own. Her parents had long ago turned over the business to the two of them and moved to southern Alabama's Gulf Coast to enjoy beach living.

She loved this motel and had welcomed the opportunity to run it, but ...

Randi scooted out from her headfirst-in-the-cabinet position. "Thank you for the help."

Her beagle Jasper nuzzled her arm as if to remind her about his help. "You too, boy." She rubbed his ears.

"Your ability to fix anything in this place amazes me." Michelle grabbed her purse and jacket.

"I watched my father do all the repairs for decades. With almost no guests at the motel, he didn't want to pay someone else." How many days of the week would you have guests wanting to stay in an older motel in a dying town? Not very many. "Now that things are better, I guess I could hire someone for jobs like this."

"Think about doing that. You're busy these days with other things."

"True." Even her best friend Michelle didn't know the whole story about her busy life.

"Well, I'm sorry you got stuck with this job. I still can't believe a guest left in the middle of the night, leaving just a message on your phone that there was a problem with the bathroom plumbing. Something about his son?"

Randi groaned. "Tell me about it. The incoming text woke me up, and it's a good thing, too, because I have a guest checking in this morning, and this is the only available cottage."

"At least the last guest left a hundred-dollar bill for repairs."

"There is that." Randi glanced over at the pipes she'd been working on. "Ancient plumbing doesn't do me any favors, either."

"Well, my husband..." Michelle giggled. "I still can't believe I get to say that. He's going to be back in town this afternoon. Neither of us is any good at plumbing, but you can give us a call if you need someone to be your assistant with anything else."

"Thanks. I hope I don't need to call." In the last few hours, she had installed a new drain from the sink, and all that was left was connecting it to the existing—and from the 1930s— plumbing. A plumber would have done this job in half the time, maybe a quarter.

With plumbing that was creeping toward a hundred years old, she never knew what would happen when she worked on it. So far so good today. Now that the motel's income was consistent and she often had fully booked weekends, she should seriously consider hiring a plumber to redo all the kitchenette and bathroom pipes in the motel's cottages.

Five minutes later, her work was complete. She turned on the water under the sink, first the hot and then the cold. Everything worked—*until* she scooted back, and the shut-off valve for the cold side stayed in her hand instead of staying attached to the pipe.

Water shot out like a geyser. Randi held up her hands to keep it away, but she was drenched in seconds.

Jasper raced around barking at the firehose of water shooting into the room. With her beagle at her side, Randi raced out of the unit to the motel's water shut-off valve outside the office building. She pried open the lid to the concrete box and turned the valve.

Seconds later, the door to cottage 3 opened, and a woman wearing a robe and with wet hair peered out.

"I'll get the water back on in just a few minutes. Sorry for the inconvenience."

The woman gave a casual wave that Randi knew was anything but. Few things could ruin your morning faster than finding out mid-shower that you suddenly had no water.

"Is the office closed?" a male voice asked.

Randi looked up to see a gorgeous man, probably in his mid-thirties, with dark wavy hair and blue eyes. He wore khaki trousers and a navy polo shirt that fit his broad shoulders nicely. She barely held back the *wow* that rose to her lips. "Do you need something?"

He gestured toward the door to the motel office, which still had the closed sign up from last night. "I'm here to register, but I know I'm early."

Always looking for someone to pet him, Jasper nudged the man's hand, and the guest-to-be leaned down to rub the dog's ears.

Cottage 4's door opened, and a man with a towel wrapped around his waist stepped onto the front step. "You gonna get this back on anytime soon?"

"Just a moment, sir. Won't be long," Randi called out to him.

To the man towering over her, she said, "I'm sorry, but I have a plumbing emergency. I'll be able to help you as soon as I get that fixed. Come on, Jasper."

The dog glanced over at her as if to say *but he's petting me, and you're preoccupied.*

Randi ran back to cottage 7 and heard footsteps behind her. At first, she assumed they were just Jasper's, but when she glanced over her shoulder, she found her new guest with Jasper beside him.

At the cottage's door, she stopped and turned toward the man. "I'm really sorry, but I can't help you right now."

"Actually, I wondered if I could help you. I'm not a plumber by any means, but I am pretty handy."

She didn't even hesitate. "Come on in. I've got to cut off this section of pipe, solder on a new one, and get everything connected before I have an outright mutiny on my hands."

As they entered the building, he asked, "Shouldn't you call a plumber?"

"I'm used to doing everything myself. Besides, one wouldn't get here before all my guests checked out in frustration."

She realized she'd been rude since he'd arrived and might also lose *him* as a guest. "I'd extend my hand, but I've been working on plumbing for hours. I'm Randi Hollis."

"John Morgan."

"Let's get this fixed. I don't want the motel's good online reputation ruined because someone's pet shark needed a swim."

He stared at her as if she'd lost her mind.

She waved him forward. "Come on. If you help me, I'll tell you the story." When they went inside, she found a half inch of water on the bathroom floor. She pulled the towels off the towel bar and threw them on the floor to sop up what they could. Then she went back to work under the sink.

As she began her task, she said, "I've had enough. I'm calling plumbers this week for quotes to modernize the plumbing."

He anticipated her need and handed her the correct wrench before she'd even asked for it. "The shark?"

"This is going to be funny in the future, but it isn't yet." She worked for a moment, then continued. "From the frantic message I received around two o'clock in the morning, it seems my guest's five-year-old son has a small stuffed shark that he adores. Unfortunately, last night, they watched something about salmon returning to the sea, and their child decided that his shark needed to return, too. The only way the boy saw to do that was to push him down the sink because water went down, and he figured it eventually had to go to the sea."

"Sounds like a smart plan to me."

She glanced over at him and saw a smiling Mr. Morgan squeezing water from a sopping wet towel into the tub and then wiping the floor with it.

"Only to the point where the shark got stuck, and Dad, being much better at some other profession than anything to do with plumbing, needed to get it out. My assumption is that the child was screaming at the top of his lungs at about this point." Randi connected a plastic pipe to what she'd replaced earlier and attached it to the old metal pipe that exited the building. "So there's a serrated knife in the kitchenette that was apparently sharp enough to cut through plastic pipes."

"You're kidding."

"Nope."

"He didn't just unscrew it and check inside the pipe?"

"No again. I immediately hurried over after I received his

text and have been here ever since then completely re-plumbing this sink. I thought I was done." She shrugged. "I think maybe I am now. You want to give that a look? See if there's anything obvious I've missed."

Randi stepped to the side, and the mirror caught her attention. "Oh no."

Her hair wasn't wet in that sultry way a magazine ad used to sell perfumes and things like that, with hair smoothly slicked back and delicate droplets of water on her skin.

Her hair was somehow in knotted ringlets. She had heaven only knew what streaked across her chin, cheek, and nose. Maybe worse than that was the sleepshirt with yellow ducks on a navy background that she'd had on when the message arrived in the night, now hung from her shoulders in a soggy mess.

Randi shrieked and heard a thunk.

"You okay?" He scooted out, rubbing the back of his head.

She ran her fingers through her hair, making it worse. At least she'd thought to pull on jeans before running out the door. And she'd given the ducks on the shirt somewhere to swim to. She giggled, and her guest gave her the side eye.

"I'm fine. Just fine." Randi eyed the pipes that had caused her sleepless night. "Would you mind staying here while I go turn the water back on? Just shout from the front door if water is still going everywhere."

"Absolutely."

Jasper, the traitor, stayed behind with Mr. Morgan while Randi hurried back to the office. Two cottage doors were open with guests looking around.

"Just a moment more. I hope," she called to them as she jogged past.

She turned on the water and waited to see Mr. Morgan step out the door. When he didn't, she started to get hopeful and ran back.

"Everything okay?"

"Nothing happened."

"Let me turn on the water here, and let's see if that continues." She twisted the knob on the hot and then the cold, and thankfully, her repair held. She stood and turned on the faucets.

John ducked under the sink. "I'm running my hand over the plumbing. It's all dry."

Her first good news of the day. She went to the middle of the parking area and shouted, "Water's fixed. Sorry for the inconvenience."

When she turned back, John came out the door, wiping his hands on his pants. "It looks like we managed to sop up all the water, but you're going to want to leave the windows open to dry this place out."

"Good idea."

"By the way, is this my cabin?" The hesitation in his voice was accompanied by a smile.

"I think it is."

Mr. Morgan grinned. "At least I know the plumbing works."

Randi couldn't help but smile back.

"I'd like to grab some breakfast. Where do you recommend?"

"Dinah's Place." She didn't bother to tell him it was the town's only restaurant.

"Okay. I'll let you clean up. Then I'll be back to check in." As she was unlocking the office, she realized that could have two meanings. The cottage needed work, but so did she. As soon as she put the cottage back as it should be, a shower was next on her list.

CHAPTER TWO

John opened the door to the scents of baking bread and chicken soup, along with the clanking of silverware. The same brown-haired waitress who'd helped him this morning directed him to a table in the middle of the room. As he walked toward the table, he realized it was the last open table in the place, so at least he'd timed his visit right.

If lunch was anything as good as breakfast had been, he knew he was in for a treat.

A man in a police uniform stopped beside his table and scanned the room. *"Nothing."*

"Everything okay?" John asked.

"Oh, sorry to interrupt you," the officer said. "I got here just a minute too late, I guess, for an empty table. It isn't usually this busy on a Tuesday."

John gestured at one of the three empty chairs at his table. "You're welcome to join me if you'd like. I'm eating alone."

The man pulled out the chair opposite him. "That would be great. I could eat in my car, but I have to tell you, that gets tiring after a while."

"Local police?"

"I'm the Two Hearts sheriff. Greg Brantley." He extended his hand over the table.

"John Morgan." They shook.

"A piece of me wants to have a casual conversation and ask what brings you to our town? But I know that'll sound like I'm grilling you when it comes out of my mouth."

John laughed. "I'll save you the grilling. I'm driving north from my winter in Florida. I had family in Two Hearts a very long time ago, so I wanted to see the town while I was nearby."

"I don't recall any Morgans around here."

"My family was the Cartwrights."

Greg's brow furrowed as he considered. "I'm sorry, but I still don't recognize the name."

"This was well over a hundred years ago."

Greg laughed. "I definitely wasn't around then. Even my mother—who knows everyone—can't claim to remember so far back."

"They owned an inn on a lake."

"Really? That's been closed as long as I've been alive—longer than that."

"That's what my research told me."

"Are you considering buying it? Because I've been through the building, and I think anyone brave enough to try is going to get a giant money pit—not to throw off your game or take away a commission from our local real estate agent."

John laughed. "No, I'm pretty handy in fixing up small projects, but I don't have any desire to take that on. Besides, I'm a writer, so refurbishing an inn doesn't fit into my life. But my great-great grandparents were the original owners of the inn—the ones who built it. I just wanted to see the town I heard about in stories from my grandparents, who heard it from them."

Greg nodded. "It's a shame when old buildings like that one

are left unoccupied, and the grounds get completely overgrown."

"I agree. It's unfortunate." Maybe if his ancestor—whom John had heard was a bit of a scoundrel—hadn't bet the inn during a poker game then lost it, he would have passed it down in the family.

The waitress, whose name tag read "Michelle," came over to take their order. The chicken and dumplings special was responsible for the scent as he entered and sounded great, so he chose that. Greg ordered his usual, whatever that was.

As they waited, Greg asked, "This is just a simple question, even though it's going to sound as if I'm giving you the third degree. How long are you staying?"

John leaned back in his chair. How long *was* he staying? His plan had been to explore the town and be on his way. He'd stick with that. "I'll be gone by the end of the week."

Greg's phone rang, and he answered it with a sigh. After hanging up, he gulped down his coffee. "My lunch has been cut short. Five head of cattle are wandering the highway. I need to direct traffic while the farmer loads them onto a truck." Greg caught Michelle's attention and asked her to make his meal to go.

Turning back to face John, Greg said, "I'm sorry to eat and run. It was nice meeting you, John."

"You too, Greg."

Greg stood when Michelle dropped off his bagged lunch. "I have to leave, but I'll see if I can get back in for a slice of pie later. You sure you don't want to stay in Two Hearts a little longer?"

John opened his mouth to say *I'll be leaving in a couple of days, three at most*, but he just couldn't say the words. "I'll think about it."

Greg gave a nod. "That's better than no. We like seeing the town grow. And you? Well, someone our age—" He chuckled as he was walking away, and John thought he heard something about "making" something and the word "match."

~

A voice he thought he recognized said, "Rats! No empty tables."

John turned in his chair to see who it was. A pretty woman he didn't recognize stood there.

Michelle's quick response of "Not a one. There's barely an empty chair" had John speak up.

"I'm almost done. You can sit with me." He added, "Greg just left," so he sounded helpful but not interested. Because he was just passing through town, not looking for a relationship.

The woman and Michelle turned toward him.

After another glance around the room, the woman came over to his table. "If you're sure?"

Michelle set down the coffee pot she'd been holding and pulled out her order pad. "Randi will keep you company."

Randi? There couldn't be two women with that unusual name in a town this size. He realized he'd been staring when she didn't sit down. "I'm positive. Sorry. I didn't recognize you." The woman in front of him with dark brown hair pulled back in a ponytail, a yellow t-shirt, and jeans paired with a nervous smile didn't resemble the woman he'd met earlier.

After a glance around the room, probably to make sure a freed-up table hadn't appeared, she sat down. "I may have been a wreck this morning." She smoothed her hands over her hair.

Michelle glanced from one to the other. "You've already met?"

"Mr. Morgan is staying at the motel." Randi rattled off an order to Michelle without checking the menu. She sipped on a cup of coffee as she waited for her meal, but she was unexpectedly quiet based on their earlier time together.

As they ate, Randi said, "Well, Mr. Morgan—"

"John, please."

"John. I'd ask if you're enjoying your stay, but you've only been here a few hours, and some of that time was spent acting as an impromptu plumber, so the answer may be no"

He laughed. "I decided to drive around the area for a while. I'll be back to check in at the usual time."

"Checking in early didn't work out, did it?" She smiled. "Sorry about that."

He waved her comment away. "No problem."

"You're here for a visit, so I guess you're on vacation."

"Not really. My work travels with me."

"What do you do?"

"I write."

"Interesting. I read." She gave a cheeky grin. "What do you write?"

"A little of this and a little of that." He continued the banter.

When Randi raised an eyebrow, John held in a smile. There was no way she was going to let him get away with half an answer.

"I mostly write mysteries, but I used to be a journalist and wrote hundreds of articles. I still like to dabble in nonfiction from time to time for fun."

"Have I read any of your mysteries? John Morgan doesn't ring a bell."

"Because of my more serious articles, I chose to write my books under a pen name. I used my mother's last name—Pearson."

"John Pearson?" Randi gave a slow nod. "I've definitely read your books. In fact, I've probably read every book you've ever written."

John grinned. Nothing about that got old. He loved knowing that the books he spent so many hours writing were enjoyed by the readers on the other end.

When they'd finished their meals, Randi said, "Michelle is

about to come back and ask you a very important question. 'Do you want dessert?'"

He started to shake his head because he tried to eat a healthy diet with only occasional sweets, but Randi added, "*No* is the wrong answer. You always want pie when you're at Dinah's."

"That good?"

"Better. All of Dinah's pies are amazing. But there's an issue now because you have to make a big decision. Do you want pie, or do you want a cupcake from Simone's? I live here, so I can balance things out. I don't need to work both in on a tight timeline. But you, you're a guest, and you need to experience it all."

John grinned. "That is tough. What if I have pie for lunch and get a cupcake I can have later with dinner? Best of both worlds."

"That's an excellent plan." Randi sat back in her chair, smiling.

Michelle came over with the coffee pot in hand. "Coffee and pie?"

"I've been told I shouldn't miss the pie."

"Randi gives good advice. Today we have chocolate cream, lemon meringue, and a peach pie that is, quite frankly, not to be missed."

"Well, I'm in peach country in the South, so I think I'd better go with the peach."

"Excellent choice. Coffee?"

John slid his cup toward her. He considered his stay in Two Hearts as Michelle got his pie. The beauty of his career was that he could literally do his job from any location that had electricity for his laptop and a decent internet connection.

That had him in Miami, Florida, last winter, and now he was on his way north to Michigan to visit a cousin who owned a boat. Both of them loved going out on the water, so he'd have fun on the water every chance he could—once he'd gotten in his writing for the day.

But there was really nothing to stop him from spending more time in Two Hearts. His family's ties to the town were tenuous at best because so many generations had passed since someone related to him had lived here. But still, the buildings on Main Street that he'd passed on his way into town had been here when they had. His great-great-grandparents had most likely been inside them to patronize the shops. And he guessed that many of the houses in this town had been here then too.

He had history here. To someone who'd moved around often for his father's job—usually from one large city to another—connection to a specific place felt good. Besides, the people had been incredibly friendly so far. After living in cities, it felt good to be in a small town.

He'd think about it—after he finished what had turned out to be amazing peach pie. Juicy and flavorful, with a sprinkling of sugar across the top crust that made it crisp when he cut into it with his fork and took his first bite.

Dinah could bake a pie, that was for sure.

"Randi, have you been here long enough to know the town well?"

She laughed, and he liked the sound. "I was born here. Do you have a question?"

He was about to ask if she knew anything about the inn when Michelle brought their checks.

"I'm sure Randi could give you a great tour of the town," the waitress added with a smile toward Randi, whose face turned beet-red.

He didn't know how to respond. She was fun to be around, but not everyone had a flexible job like his. "I don't want to impose." He immediately hated how formal that sounded.

Michelle added, "I happen to know she's often free this time of day."

It didn't seem as if he had a choice, and he wouldn't mind spending more time with Randi, so he gave in. "In that case, I would like to have a tour."

When they left the restaurant, instead of going toward his truck, Randi veered right and started down the sidewalk. "Let's walk."

The bright blue sky and temperatures in the warm but not too hot category had him following her suggestion. Besides, he'd end up gaining weight if he stayed here longer and kept eating like this. Exercise needed to be his close friend.

He'd come back to get his truck and get take-out for dinner. It seemed he had two options for dinner while he was at the motel: take-out from Dinah's or fix something he'd buy during the grocery store's open hours.

He enjoyed cooking, but working in the cottage's tiny kitchenette wasn't ideal. For this short visit, he'd buy some lunch meat, bread, and toppings for easy dinners. He'd had that meal dozens of times before when he was on the road, and he would certainly survive. Or he could drive to wherever an open restaurant *could* be found.

Right now, he planned to focus on his tour guide.

CHAPTER THREE

Randi pointed out a few things as they walked. When they arrived at the area of the road with old storefronts, she said, "Downtown was dead not long ago." The brick buildings had historic charm. But the town seemed alive, so he found her comment hard to believe.

Then he realized that, even though some stores were open for business, quite a few buildings still looked empty.

As they passed a photography studio, the woman inside waved at them, and Randi waved back. After a second's pause, the woman gleefully picked up her phone. When Randi saw it happen, she sighed with what he'd have to call frustration.

"That's Paige. She opened her bridal photo studio a few months ago."

He waited for an explanation about her sigh, but when she didn't continue, he decided he must have imagined it.

They continued on. A building across the street with a bow window featured a "Coming Soon" banner for a bookstore. The *Two Hearts Times* newspaper already seemed to be open above it.

"The town can't be doing too badly if it has a newspaper."

Randi laughed. "Amy recently revived it."

"I'm starting to pick up the trend."

Something in the front window moved. Maybe a cat. It was brown and fluffy with … long ears? "Is that a rabbit?" he asked incredulously.

Randi nodded. "Amy sometimes takes her pet rabbit to work. That's Nosey."

He needed to be more polite. "I'm sorry. I didn't mean to be rude."

She giggled. "The rabbit is *named* Nosey."

He smiled back.

Elaborate bridal gowns were displayed in the window of the building next door. The sign said "Wedding Bella," so this was yet one more business focused on weddings. He didn't bother to ask the business's age because the sign hanging in front had a fresh newness to it even though the wedding store was housed in an old brick building.

"Bella owns the wedding dress store. She just had a baby who is so sweet. We could go into Wedding Bella as part of your tour if you want."

A store filled with wedding dresses and women cooing over a baby? "I think it's better to keep the tour simple this time." He thought that had sounded like a good excuse for not going in there.

Randi nodded. "Can't handle that much girly stuff at one time?"

He laughed. "You knew that when you mentioned it, didn't you?"

"I may have." She grinned. "We'll keep going to the bakery. But Rose is a cute baby." Thankfully, Randi changed the subject. "Are you working on a new book while you're here?"

"I'm almost always writing. This book isn't in my Peter O'Keefe detective series. It's going to be a standalone thriller."

She grinned. "I'm looking forward to it. Does this book take place in Florida? I've been there a few times."

"Yes." Should it? He'd struggled to give this story a tropical feel. "It might be fun to write one that takes place here."

"I don't usually change the setting once I've started writing." He considered that as he walked. "But I may need to do that this time." He'd already been in situations and had seen things here that he could use. Even though he'd only driven into this town today, setting the book in Two Hearts felt right. And he could include a lot of what he learned in the next few days. Maybe the many sweet treats would find their way into a crime. "Thanks for your suggestion. I think I may move it to here."

"Oh! That makes me even more excited to read this book."

On his side of the street, he passed what looked like a commercial kitchen. Then they stopped in front of a bakery with a pink door, which must belong to Simone.

Randi stared at the bakery, then turned to face him with her arms crossed in front of her chest. "This may not be the good idea I thought it was earlier." She gestured with her shoulder toward the window display which screamed weddings. A three-tiered cake featuring a contemporary bride and groom topper sat next to cupcakes with monogrammed tops.

"I live here and am used to everything having to do with weddings. My motel is thriving now because of them. But, if we walk through this door together, rumors will fly."

This town seemed to love all things wedding. As a happy single man, that should make him drive out of here as fast as his truck could go, but he was content in his current single state.

"I doubt it's that bad."

Randi's eyes widened. "Have you ever lived in a small town?"

"Never."

She stared at him. "Small towns can pass information like lightning."

"But is anyone watching us to start this rumor?"

She laughed. "Everyone knows you're here by now. A

handsome man, who by all signs seems to be single, drove into town alone. And he's a famous author. They're going to be looking for someone to match you up with."

"Handsome?"

She raised her hands in mock frustration. "That's all you heard?"

"I'm not concerned about the rumors." A bell rang as he opened the door. "Besides, I doubt anyone actually cares about our situation."

Randi started to follow him, then stopped and grabbed his sleeve. "Wait," she whispered. "I can't go in here. That's one of the town's biggest gossips."

A woman his mother's age stood at the counter talking to a woman closer to his own who was wearing an apron—pink, of course. The older woman seemed to be ordering a cake.

When he didn't say anything, Randi whispered, "I can't get caught up in matchmaking again. If you have any questions about the town, I'll be at the motel for a while this afternoon." She slinked out of the place, giving a backward glance as she stepped onto the sidewalk, apparently to make sure she hadn't been spotted.

John surveyed the options in the glass case. He currently had his choice of chocolate or lemon. Either would work, but neither was a true favorite. They still looked delicious.

"Hello, young man. Are you just visiting Two Hearts?" the woman Randi had labeled a gossip asked him as she folded a receipt and tucked it into her purse.

"Yes, ma'am." Randi must be wrong because she didn't seem to know anything about him.

"Planning to stay past your Friday checkout?"

John fought a laugh. So much for his earlier conclusion. "I haven't decided."

She looked him up and down as though assessing his assets. "I'm sure you'll be welcome here if you choose to stay a while."

He grinned. "Thank you."

She gave a single nod, then turned and left.

He should have credited Randi with knowing her town. He'd do his best to stay off the radar, not because he felt threatened but because it would just make life easier.

The proprietress eyed him. "Welcome to my bakery. Are you in town for a wedding?"

"Just—." He started to say *passing through,* but that didn't sit right. Maybe he had already made a decision.

"I'm thinking about staying for a while."

She smiled widely. "Well, then, welcome to Two Hearts. I'm Simone."

"John. But I won't be staying permanently."

"We'll try to change your mind." Simone grinned again. "Now," she turned to business, "I assume you're here for a cupcake?"

At his nod, she continued. "I have the chocolate and lemon in the case. But I also just finished frosting some carrot cake cupcakes with cream cheese frosting."

"Sold," he said immediately.

"No hesitation? You don't want to take a moment to consider the others?" she asked in a cheeky way.

"Carrot cake is my absolute favorite. It's going to be hard for me to not buy more than one, but I just had really good pie."

She laughed. "Well, it kind of depends on what you're going to have for dinner. Maybe get in some veggies to balance everything out."

"I know I either have to go back to Dinah's Place or go out of town for dinner. Are there many options?"

"You can get most anything within about a thirty- to forty-five-minute drive. My favorite is the pizza place, though. They make a great veggie pizza. And if you don't already know, Dinah isn't open for dinner."

He blew out a breath. "That does make evenings more complicated." John shrugged. "But I haven't had pizza for a while."

"Here." She reached under the cash register stand and pulled out a piece of paper. "Amy, the newspaper's owner, put together an information sheet for visitors. And let me circle," she said, pulling out a pen, "the pizza parlor. If you put the address in your phone, it'll be really easy to find."

Simone handed him a box with two cupcakes. "The second one is on the house. I hope you enjoy your stay in Two Hearts."

"I know I'm going to enjoy it, but I'm definitely going to have to pace myself on sweets."

Simone leaned an elbow against the glass bakery case. "Where are you going to live while you're here?"

"The motel is fine." He couldn't cook much, but he'd survive. "I'll extend my stay for a month or two."

She shook her head. "Not possible."

A small town couldn't be that busy. "Do they have a limit on length of stay?"

She laughed. "*Weddings.*"

Simone spoke the word as if it said it all.

"Excuse me? I've noticed a love of weddings here, but ..."

"Two Hearts loves weddings because they brought the town back to life. We're a destination wedding location. I happen to know there will be a big wedding in Two Hearts this weekend because I'm doing the cake."

He stared at her, waiting for her to explain the connection to the motel. "And that means I can't stay at the motel past Friday?"

"Every cottage at the motel will be booked. I can guarantee that. But maybe there was a cancellation." Her voice suggested that wouldn't be likely. "You should check with Randi."

The idea of spending time with Randi again brought a smile to his face.

Simone watched him for a moment before saying, "You've met her?"

John remembered Randi's caution about gossips and matchmakers. "She checked me into the motel."

"*Right.*" She stretched out the word, clearly believing there was more to the story.

"Maybe there's another motel not far away."

"Not one you want to stay at. Let's just say law enforcement is a frequent visitor there. But maybe you could rent a house for a month or two."

He loved a simple solution. "That might work. I'll think about it."

Simone cocked her head to the side. "You're not going to find a job here. You know that, right?"

He laughed. "I'm a writer, so I can work almost anywhere."

"Oh. Have you written anything I might have read?"

"That depends on what you like to read."

"Romance?"

He laughed. "Definitely not my genre. I'm mystery and thriller." He picked up his cupcakes. "I'm sure I'll see you around."

"I'm your destination for cakes if you need one. Especially wedding cakes."

He took a step back. "I am definitely not in the market for a wedding cake."

She leaned toward him. "Oh, it sounds like there's a story there."

He lifted his shoulder in a shrug. "Not really. I just haven't found anybody I wanted to marry."

"That's fair. I hadn't myself either until earlier this year."

As he returned to Dinah's, where he'd left his truck, he

munched on a delicious cupcake. The buildings he passed looked completely different to him now.

Before, he'd seen the street as part of a dying town with only a few shops left open. But now he knew it was a town that was coming alive again with these new shops and new people trusting Two Hearts for their livelihood. But he wouldn't be buying a wedding cake to help support the bakery.

CHAPTER FOUR

Randi sat at her desk with a sigh. She'd taken precious time away from her already busy workday to show John some of Two Hearts. She should regret that but just couldn't.

Yesterday, he'd just been a guest passing through town. A kind one because he'd helped her when he didn't have to.

Nice. But just passing through.

Now, she'd spent more time with him and liked him. Maybe more than she should for someone who wouldn't be here in a week.

Her phone rang with a call from Michelle.

"I managed to squeeze in an afternoon break. I can come over and help if you're still working on that sink project. Sam said he'd help too."

"I finished that up not long after you left."

"I wondered about you being at Dinah's—and no longer looking like a drowned rat—but I couldn't slow down long enough to ask. I'm surprised you did it without an assistant."

Randi picked up a pen and flipped it back and forth in her hand.

"Tell me his name," Michelle said with a no-nonsense tone when Randi remained silent.

Randi laughed. "A guest checking in saw my distress and stepped in to help." That covered the situation nicely. *If Michelle didn't read between the lines.*

"That handsome guest you were sitting with at lunch?"

That's what happened when you'd known your best friend forever. "He didn't offer because he was handsome—notice how I'm not ignoring that because it's obvious. He stepped out of his pickup as I was trying to turn off the water to the motel."

"Water? To the whole motel? Wow. I'm sorry I had to leave when you needed me."

"It's okay. Everything's working now."

"Then he asked you to lunch." Michelle's romantic sigh came through the line.

"Then I got out of there as quickly as I could because I was drenched and dirty. That's why John didn't recognize me at first. I showered, finished my morning work, and went to get lunch *by myself*. Remember that Greg was sitting with him before I arrived."

"I forgot. But you left with him." Her hopeful tone of voice made Randi chuckle.

"You forced me into it," Randi said with a laugh.

"Right. I forgot."

"And what happened to your first rule? Never date anyone who isn't planning to stay here. I've always thought that was sound advice."

"I know. I know. Stick with the rule. It can be difficult, though."

"It's *your* rule!"

"I just want you to be happy. But I found my husband by breaking that rule."

"I still think it's wise. I don't need heartbreak from a visitor."

Michelle sighed. "Our many visitors are both the blessing

and the downside of our town right now. We do have people coming, including this handsome guy, but they spend just enough time here to go to a wedding or get a bite to eat at the diner, and then they keep on going."

It was Randi's turn to sigh. "You're right. Your guy stayed around because he needed to heal from an accident."

Michelle laughed. "So true. You'll have to figure out a way to keep John here if you're interested."

"I won't let myself become interested." Her heart said, *Really? Are you sure you haven't already done that?*

She ignored it.

Randi heard the restaurant's door chime, and Michelle said, "A group of tourists just came in. Talk to you later." Michelle ended the call.

Randi stared at her desk, exhaustion threatening to overtake her. She knew she should do something other than just sit here, but she felt like she needed a break. After the plumbing situation that had her with a wrench in her hand at dawn and the walk with John, she was ready for a nap.

She opened the file folder in front of her, and the list inside brought a smile to her face and re-energized her. Her secret project, the one only Albert at the hardware store knew about, required a strict timeline.

It was silly to keep the project to herself, but she felt like others would try to talk her out of it. If she didn't tell anyone, she could make her dream happen.

She'd kept her secret as she'd cleaned up over half of the Two Hearts Inn's thirty guest rooms. After half a century of being abandoned, everything had taken a lot of work. Four of those had even been painted. But she had plans for more. *So much more.*

Randi fingered the list. Every time she came up with something a guest at the inn might enjoy, she wrote it on this page. She could have put it on a computer spreadsheet, but being able to hold the list in her hands made her dream seem more real. Everything from rowboats on the lake to nighttime stargazing was here.

Electricity was at the top of the list. As the real estate agent for the inn, she knew that would help find a buyer *and* help her as she worked on the property. She'd once asked the absentee owner if he would have the power turned on. He'd ranted for ten minutes about how much the inn cost already with property taxes and how he wasn't going to spend another penny on the money pit.

The sound of a text arriving had her check her phone. Albert had more paint for her. When custom colors didn't turn out right for a customer, the can of paint would be sold at a discount, and she needed all the discounts she could find. He'd had some last week that had gone on the walls of a guest room.

In six months, maybe less, if she could sell more houses and add to her growing savings account, the inn could be hers. Of course, she'd need more money to do all the work that was needed, but she'd figure that out later.

One step at a time. Right now, that meant she needed to go to the hardware store.

CHAPTER FIVE

Randi drove past the lake park, then CJ and Paige's pink Victorian house before curving around the lake on the road that circled it. Most of the houses beside the lake were abandoned from when the town had been dead for decades. A couple had owners who'd been there for generations, but the only one that had been sold since the town started attracting interest was the one her friends owned.

It hadn't been in her lifetime that they talked about a hot spring being here, but fifty, sixty, maybe more years ago, there had been one. It had been behind the Victorian inn on the lake, a place that celebrities and other people with the means to afford it had come to "take the waters," as they said then, for their supposed healing powers.

For some unknown reason, the spring had dried up—and so had the town. The inn was the hardest hit, though, because the loss of that attraction had meant almost no one wanted to stay there. Her family's motel had survived because it was less expensive to maintain. She remembered that her father did handyman work for others, too, when she was young, so they must have been barely getting by at the motel.

The amazing view of the lake from the windows on the back of the inn hadn't changed. But the view alone hadn't been enough for potential guests. And that brought her to today.

Randi turned down the long drive that, when cleared of debris and vines—decades of overgrowth—would lead to the covered portico at the front of the inn. When the inn had first opened, ladies would step down from a horse-drawn carriage there. Then it became a car or truck. She knew from old photos that the driveway curved around the front of the building to form a circular drive, but that was lost inside a tangled mess.

She should probably have a real estate sign out front, but what would be the point? The inn was for sale and could easily be found online. Besides, a sign would cost her money, and for a building with little chance of selling, it would be a waste of that money.

The first section of the driveway remained mostly clear of the brush and weeds that had overtaken the rest of the property. Probably because the sheriff routinely came out to make sure things were in decent condition and that there were no squatters—or teenagers who came out here occasionally to park.

"Okay, boy, it's time to go inside. Are you ready?"

Jasper wagged his tail back and forth. The inn was much bigger than her owner's quarters at the motel, so Jasper got to play with his ball inside, bringing him no end of joy.

The two of them made their way through the brush and vines that covered the path to the front of the building, Jasper often dashing ahead then coming back to make sure she was okay.

She'd been a real estate agent for close to a year now, and there had been a few inquiries on this old building, but as soon as she explained the state of the property, they said, "No, thank you."

At first, she'd been frustrated because she'd have received a good commission if it had sold. The property may not be going for top value at this point, but it would still sell for a lot more than one of the houses in town.

Then she'd had a change of heart.

Maybe it was because she'd spent time out here looking around and getting a feel for what the inn had been and could be again. She'd snapped photos for each of the potential buyers because they'd asked different questions.

Before long, she could picture herself at that elegantly carved wooden front desk, checking in guests.

She already ran a motel. Sure, this was bigger, and it would come with more challenges. It was also about half a century older than her motel—maybe even a little more. But it was absolutely beautiful.

She wished she could make an offer on it today, but that just wasn't possible. She had to keep saving her money.

Randi unlocked the door, and they went in.

As always, she took a moment to admire this place. Ceilings stretched twenty-six feet high above her. The room somehow elegantly mixed rustic wood beams and a slate floor with details like deep-brown mahogany carved with whimsical and intricate designs and a massive crystal chandelier she knew would be gorgeous once the cobwebs and grime were removed.

Randi took Jasper's ball out and rolled it in the direction of the ballroom. No furniture remained downstairs except for the built-in pieces. She wasn't sure how the chandeliers had escaped being sold, but maybe there just wasn't a need around here for something that large when everything had gone up for auction.

Her phone chimed, so she checked it, frowning at what she found. A man who had contacted her last week asking for information about the land the inn sat on was back and wanted more details and photos. Second inquiries often meant more than passing interest, but so far, no one had been willing to take on this renovation. Only her.

She crossed the lobby and went up the stairs. It had an elevator, but even after the electricity to the inn was turned back on, no one in their right mind would try to get that engine started and step inside the box without an escape plan. After all this time, she'd have to get a historic elevator expert to come out from Nashville.

Randi reached the top of the wide stairway which curved elegantly toward the second floor, then stood to admire the lobby. Even in its current state, she knew it could be brought back to life. The ground floor level remained in the state she'd found it, but she'd cleaned the upstairs a little at a time over the last four months. If sales kept up with real estate and bookings at her motel, she'd be able to buy the inn by the end of the year.

She just hoped no one else would want it before then because a little piece of her heart would break. She had spent endless hours of sweat equity on this place. The inn had thirty rooms, and she had cleaned sixteen and a half of them. She'd even painted a few.

Today, it should become seventeen if no one needed her with either of her other businesses.

Jasper raced up the stairs with his ball in his mouth and walked beside her, apparently wanting to know where Mom was going to be while he played.

Two hours later, Randi stood and stretched her back, wishing she could wash up. She'd worn rubber gloves, but that hadn't protected her arms or her face. She had a tendency to get dirt everywhere. Michelle would be pristine and clean after a project, but Randi would be a mess.

This place hadn't had power or running water for a very long time. She pulled out a wet wipe to get off the majority of the mess and gathered up her cleaning supplies, always careful not to leave anything behind.

It wasn't that she was doing anything wrong, though, because she knew the owner would be quite happy if the place were cleaner and showed better. And if a potential buyer ever came upstairs, they might see the potential the old girl had now that most of the rooms were clean.

CHAPTER SIX

The veggie pizza had been good, just as Simone had said it would be. That had all gone well. John just wasn't sure where he was right now.

In an effort to see more of the area, he'd started driving around. Dusk had come, and then it had gotten dark. He'd like to say he was the man who had a perfect sense of direction and always knew where he was, but that would be a lie.

He had been in what was clearly the town, with house after house, some looking more lived in than others, more cared for, and then he'd left that and curved around to some large houses in a row after what looked like a park. Now that it was dark, all he saw was trees lit by his headlights and moonlight. If he didn't find signs of civilization soon, he'd have to turn around to get back to where he'd started.

Of course, he could bring up the map on his phone, but what was the fun in that? Sometimes, life needed to go in unexpected directions.

Something light-colored darted across the road in front of him, and he slammed on the brakes, stopping just before he hit it.

John got out of the car, and a little dog looked up at him. A corgi, he thought.

"What are you doing out here at night?"

She woofed.

Then she looked over to the side of the road like she was about to make a run for it. His headlights shone off of her, and he could see a pink collar and a tag hanging off it.

"I think you must live around here, and I am guessing that your mom and dad don't know where you are right now."

She cocked her head to the side and gave him a stare that said, *You're probably right, but how did you figure that out?*

He took a step toward her and then another, waiting to see if she'd snap at him or run away. When she wagged her tail so hard her whole body shook, he reached down tentatively and petted her head.

"You're a sweetheart, aren't you?" When she kept wagging her tail, he scooped her up in his arms and looked around. Darkness had swallowed everything, with faint moonlight and his headlights lending the only light. Then he noticed a driveway to his right.

"Is that where you're from?"

She swiped her tongue across his chin.

Laughing, John said, "I don't know if that's *yes* or just *thank you for saving me.* Why don't we get in the car, and I'll pull in that driveway. We'll go see if that's where you're from. I don't want you to get hit by a car."

As he pulled in, his headlights caught the glint of metal and color. Driving slowly up the narrow drive, he soon realized it was the back of a vehicle.

"It looks like somebody's home." Before he got out, he turned on his truck's overhead light to check her tag. "I should have done this sooner." He sighed in frustration. "Unfortunately, it doesn't have your name on it. It just says that you've had your shots. Let's go see if this is your house." He opened the door while holding on to her collar and then scooped her up into his arms again.

That's when he realized that there may be a vehicle here, but there weren't other signs that someone lived there, not even a cleared path to the door.

He started to the left and had to crouch down in a few places to avoid being hit by branches. When he finally came out of the nasty, overgrown path, he found himself standing in front of a massive building that was dark inside except for a faint light coming through one of the upstairs windows.

"Maybe a hermit lives here. Anyone else would have cleared a decent path to the driveway."

A piece of him wondered if this was *the* inn, but he dismissed the idea immediately. This grand old building did not resemble the stories he'd been told. That building had been twice this size in the stories his grandfather had told.

John got to the door and didn't see a doorbell of any kind, so he knocked on it, and it creaked open.

"Hello, is anybody home? Your door opened when I knocked on it."

He heard the skittering of feet on the floor and got ready to run because it sounded like a pack of bloodhounds was after him. Then, a beagle with a blue-and-white-striped collar John recognized poked its nose through the open area between the wall and the door and looked up at him.

"Jasper, is that you?"

The dog wagged his tail, and the one in John's arms squirmed. "Hey, settle down. I don't think you live here. If you did, you would probably both have been running outside, but Jasper's safely shut up inside."

Jasper started to push his body through the partially open door, but John nudged him back, not wanting to have two escaped dogs. John stepped inside and closed the door behind him.

He turned on his phone's flashlight app. found himself in a huge room with wide stairs leading to another floor in what appeared to be an abandoned mansion. When he looked to his right, he noticed what may have once been a hotel's front desk. Could this be the inn his family once owned? Maybe the family stories had become exaggerated over time. He'd tried to find information about the property before coming here but found very little.

And Jasper's presence suggested that Randi lived here.

A second later, he realized the cobwebs told him no one did.

"Hello, is anyone here?" he called out. Randi's dog was here, so she must be here, too.

When he moved closer to the stairway, he heard music playing upstairs. John set the dog he'd found on the floor, and she and Jasper raced around the room like best friends. When the sound kicked off, he shouted again.

"Hello? Randi?"

As he waited, he checked out the room. This had been spectacular in its day. Even draped with what must be decades of cobwebs, the crystal light fixture added an elegant touch.

Randi's face, lit by the battery-powered lantern in her hand, hesitantly peered around the corner at the top of the stairs.

"I wanted to see if this dog was yours." He pointed to the corgi as it dashed by with Jasper.

Randi stepped fully into view.

"She ran in front of my car, and I saw the driveway, so I wanted to see if she belonged here."

Randi glanced from him to the dogs and back over at him before starting down the stairs. "You startled me. I didn't expect anyone else to be here."

"I knocked on the door, and it opened." He felt like he needed to explain again now that she could actually hear him.

"I'm going to need to have a locksmith repair that. It isn't securely closing unless I lock the deadbolt, and that only works from outside."

When she got halfway down the stairs, she said, "That's Daisy. She belongs to Paige and CJ. They're not far away in the pink house on the lake."

He shrugged. "I can't tell house color at night. Pink can hide in the darkness. And that's saying a lot with all the pink in this town."

She started down the stairs.

"Do you live here?"

"Me?" She put her hand on her chest. "No one lives in the Two Hearts Inn."

The *inn*. His family's old property.

She continued, "I'm the real estate agent for the property."

"I thought you worked at the motel." How many jobs could she have?

She laughed, and she was absolutely stunning—even with a streak of dirt across her chin. "Just two. Some days, I'm dividing my time between the motel and being a real estate agent." She paused halfway down the stairs. "We can go together to return her. Unless you'd rather leave Daisy with me."

He was tired of his own company after his drive and dinner, so the idea of spending time with anyone who might have a conversation with him made John say, "Let's do this together. I'd like to meet more people."

Then he realized this might be his only chance to see the property. Even if he did stay for a month or two, there wouldn't be a legitimate reason for him to tour the inn. He definitely wouldn't be buying it. "Before we go, could I see this place? It's the old inn I read about online, right?"

She seemed startled. "You found it online looking for Two Hearts travel information? I'm surprised it popped up in a search."

"My—"

The dogs charged through the room, barely missing him.

"Jasper! Daisy! *Behave*."

Her dog skidded to a stop and looked up at her, but Daisy was still on the move. The corgi circled Jasper as if daring him to play again.

Randi checked her watch. "The inn has been abandoned for a very long time. Are you sure you want to see it?" She held up her lantern. "This is all the light I have."

"Positive." He had a family connection he'd been about to mention a moment ago, but that probably didn't matter. Besides, if he saw it now, he'd be able to picture it restored, and that *could* be a great setting. "This would be a great setting to add to my next book.

She gave a positive murmur. "I can show it to you, but I need to get out of here soon, so I'll give you the quick tour." She gestured toward the room they were in. "This is the lobby, as you can tell. It's in original condition."

He chuckled. "It definitely hasn't been touched for a while."

"I make sure there aren't any rodents or anything else hiding in here. There were some mice when I got the listing, but I rehomed them."

He nodded.

"Over here," she went to the left, "is the ballroom, and beyond that, the dining room, both on a grand scale."

John gave a low whistle when they entered the ballroom. "This must have been something when it was new." Even by the lantern, he could tell this room had great bones. The dark wood paneling halfway up the walls, paired with floral wallpaper above, gave the dining room an elegant appearance.

Randi stepped next to him and motioned toward a platform in the corner. "I can picture the early days of the inn. The gentlemen and ladies in their long dresses, music playing from a band or orchestra over there. Laughter. It must have been something special." Her enthusiasm was contagious.

She led him through a wide cased opening into the dining room. "I've seen photos of this room. There were round tables. Guests would have sat here talking about their day. Taking the waters of the spring, rowing on the lake, maybe the men sharing fishing stories."

"Fine dining with a view of the lake."

Randi nodded excitedly. "Exactly. I found some old menus tucked in the pantry. I think they're from the 1920s. Pheasant under glass. Oysters Rockefeller. Pineapple upside-down cake. Those were apparently all the rage in the 20s."

Her passion for the place wrapped around them. John could see the scene as she painted it. For a moment, when she stepped closer, he wanted to put his arm around her. *It's just the moment and her infectious excitement.*

He took a step to the side and glanced around the room. "This is what I wanted. To see what it looked like inside. It's in surprisingly good shape in here, considering what the path to get inside looked like."

Randi laughed. "One corner of the building had a tree fall on it. I had someone come out and help me close up the hole so that the inside is protected, but there will be a lot of work for a new owner."

"That door circles back around to the lobby." Randi pointed to their right. "There's a pass-through under the staircase that's hidden from the guests. It goes to the kitchen, so workers were able to bring food through without disrupting the guests. I could take you to the kitchen, but it just looks like an old, grimy kitchen.

"And there's a second floor, of course, with guest rooms and also an attic. I also rehomed three raccoons and some squirrels who'd enjoyed the access, apparently from using the fallen tree and the hole it had made as their personal entrance." She checked her phone. "Yikes! I have to get out of here. I told a client we could view a house tonight, but unless we hustle, I'm going to be very late, and I don't like that."

He looked longingly at the staircase, wanting to explore, but he knew he'd worn out his welcome for now. He scooped up Daisy and followed Randi and Jasper to the door and outside.

She jogged down the path like someone who'd been here many times, her dog keeping pace beside her.

When they arrived at their cars, he said, "I appreciate the tour."

"Follow me after we've pulled out. I'll slow down by Paige and CJ's house and flash my lights. I wish I could stay, but I really have to hurry now."

CHAPTER SEVEN

John rushed to his own vehicle to move out of the way for her. True to her word, she slowed down in front of a large Victorian house—historic details like gingerbread trim were visible with only a porch light on.

As he pulled in front of the house, he noticed Randi coming to a stop in the middle of the road. Then she did a U-turn and returned.

He climbed out of his truck, then reached back and scooped up Daisy.

Randi parked in front of him. When she got out, she said, "I called the man I was supposed to meet. He had to postpone the showing, so I thought it might be easier for you and Daisy if I came along."

The two of them walked up to the well-lit covered porch.

"I'm glad you're here." He realized he'd put too much enthusiasm into his words when she furrowed her brow. As he went over his words, he realized he enjoyed being around Randi more than he should for someone who didn't plan to stay here long. John quickly added, "You're right that it will be easier if a stranger doesn't show up alone with their dog."

Looking for a distraction, he glanced to his right, where he could make out the side of another large Victorian home. "Are there more of these houses or just these two?"

"There is a row of them along the lake, probably seven or eight. I think this was considered the fancy part of town in its heyday. These are all on the lake, just like the inn."

He processed that thought. There was something compelling about this town. He wished it was daylight so he could see everything better.

"This is the only one with the lights on. The area seems almost abandoned, for lack of a better word."

She nodded. "That's how the whole town felt not long ago. But there are only a few of these houses that are occupied. They're all in decent condition, though."

Nothing about his first day in Two Hearts had gone as he'd expected. He'd been early for his reservation and greeted by a woman who looked like she'd walked through a tornado because of the tangled, wet mess of her hair and the grime. Then he'd met her again at the restaurant and hadn't even recognized her.

He'd quickly learned that Randi wasn't anything like the windswept woman he'd first met, but there still seemed to be something about her he couldn't figure out. But he didn't think he'd be in town long enough to try.

Randi pushed the doorbell while he held onto the dog, who was now wiggling to get down.

A man opened the door and looked from Randi to him. "Daisy?"

A woman who looked vaguely familiar ran over. "Daisy rang the doorbell? How did she reach it?"

Both John and Randi laughed, then John said, "I'm the doorbell ringer. I was driving down the road exploring the town, and this little dog ran in front of my car. I stopped in time to avoid hitting her. I'm quite grateful for that. But I went to the first driveway, and that turned out to be the old inn where I found Randi."

It broke his heart to see that it was in such bad shape, even though his family had only owned it for a short time. "And she knew Daisy."

The man put out his hand. "I'm CJ MacIntosh, and this is my wife Paige. Thank you for bringing Daisy home."

Paige's brow furrowed. "I know John was driving around and ended up at the inn, but why were *you* there, Randi?"

"I'm the real estate listing agent for the inn. I was over checking on it," Randi said. "I don't like the building sitting empty, so I go over there at least once a week."

Paige breathed out a sigh. "I am so glad you said that. I've seen lights in the direction of the inn at night. I even asked Greg about it. He went over and said he didn't see evidence of squatters or anything else wrong."

Randi laughed in what John would have to describe as a self-conscious way. "I do a little routine maintenance. Making sure no critters have snuck in or windows have been broken. I can only find the time in the evenings after I've finished everything else."

The dog wiggled harder. "Should I put Daisy down? She must have gotten out somehow."

"Just a minute. Let me grab a flashlight." CJ came back with a powerful light and walked the perimeter of the fence. "There's a hole right here. I certainly hope she hasn't figured out the joys of digging and going under the fence. I'll put a few large rocks here to get us through the night."

Paige reached out her arms. "Hand her over to me, and I'll lock her inside. She can wait until CJ is done fixing her mess."

Paige looked down at the little dog, who was now in her arms. "What were you thinking? You could have been hurt. We take good care of you. You can't get better care than you do here."

Daisy licked her owner's chin just like she had John's.

To Randi and John, Paige said, "Can you stay for a minute?"

Randi looked down at herself. "I've been cleaning up a few things at the inn, so I'm sure I'm a mess."

Again, she mentioned work that seemed odd for the property's listing agent. Maybe she was extra conscientious.

Paige opened the door. "You're fine. There's always something I'm working on in this place. If you want, you can go down the hall and wash your hands. Then come, sit, and have some iced tea with us. I made a fresh batch today."

It was hard to believe, but he'd only arrived in Two Hearts this morning. This had been a long—but good—day. He was exhausted. One glance at Randi seemed to say the same thing.

"Are you just passing through, John?"

That seemed to be the standard question in this town, probably because the weddings he kept hearing about brought so many visitors. "That was my intention. It's a nice place, though. I may like to stay for just a little while longer, maybe a month or two. Simone told me there was no way I was going to get to stay at the motel too much longer."

Randi agreed. "Definitely not. I'm booked this weekend and next weekend solid."

He sighed. "Is it hard to find a rental? Maybe a house?"

Everyone except him laughed.

Paige answered. "It's more like, what kind of rental do you want? Because there are a lot of empty houses in this town. And are you willing to do any fix-up work while you're in it? Or do you want something that's in awesome shape to start with?"

"I don't mind a little work. I used to help my dad with odd projects."

"Then you can probably have your pick from about a fourth of the houses in this town." CJ added, "I lived in a rental house when I arrived in town and helped with repairs there. And I'm the town's carpenter if you end up needing one. I should say the main carpenter because I'm training a couple of guys."

Paige spoke up. "And I'm a wedding photographer, but I'll take other photos too."

"Do you own that shop on Main Street?"

"That's me," she said, grinning.

She'd been the one on the phone who appeared to be gleefully passing along information about him—and possibly Randi. But maybe he'd put that story on something innocent, like a conversation with a client. Either way, Paige seemed sweet and harmless.

"Where do I go to find a rental? I don't imagine there's a rental office in a town this small."

Paige pointed at Randi.

"She's it. Randi's the real estate agent and does the rentals too."

He stared. "Hold it. You work at the motel, you're the real estate agent, *and* you manage rentals?"

"Oh, it's more than that. I *own* the motel, and I do those other things." She laughed.

"How much would rent in Two Hearts be?" He'd just come from a small, one-bedroom apartment in Florida because anything larger came at a higher cost than he'd been willing to pay.

Randi quoted him a price.

"For a whole house? For a month? That isn't possible." He felt like they were having fun at his expense.

Without any signs of amusement, Randi said, "I know it's hard to believe, but you're a long way from the city right now. There's no major industry, and Two Hearts has just started to come alive again after a long sleep. You don't have to spend very much here."

Paige added, "It may not be luxury accommodations."

"I backpacked in the Andes. Stayed in a yurt in Mongolia for a month. And I had a charming four-story walk-up apartment in Paris. I've experienced many different ways to live. Unless it's infested with vermin, because I really, really dislike insects and rodents inside a home, I don't think there's anything in this town that would scare me."

Randi pulled out her phone and scrolled. "Are you ready to look at some places? I have openings tomorrow."

He thought about it. "Let me sleep on it."

Paige stepped in. "We're glad you're thinking about staying here. Just remember that we don't have big-city refinements. You have to drive about ninety minutes to Nashville for anything like that."

"I write books. Mystery novels. So I can live anywhere. The yurt and the backpacking trip didn't even give me internet. But I can still make notes and write longhand."

"Everywhere in Two Hearts has decent internet, so you'll be fine."

"Have I read your books?" Paige asked.

This was the standard question he was asked, but it was always difficult to answer because it mattered what they liked to read. If they only enjoyed fun romances set in small towns, probably not. But if they liked thrillers with exciting twists and turns, maybe.

"I write as John Pearson."

Paige squealed. "I love your books. You've kept me up late at night when I've heard the house creak in the wind."

"I'm not sure at this point if I should apologize."

She grinned. "Don't you dare. You write amazing books."

Daisy scratched at the door just as CJ opened it, and she raced outside.

"All fixed for now. We may need to come up with a system. Maybe putting decorative rock around the fence on all sides."

"That would be a lot of work, but I certainly don't want her to get injured." Paige motioned toward John. "He's thinking about staying in town a little while. And he writes books as John Pearson. You know, that author that has me lying in bed with my eyes wide open because I'm too scared to sleep."

CJ went to the kitchen and washed his hands. Over the water, he said, "It sounds like I missed a lot. If you need anything, John, let me know."

Randi yawned, and that was his cue to leave.

"It was a pleasure meeting both of you. I'm sure I'll see you around."

As they walked down the path to their cars, he said to Randi, "The part of the inn I saw looked beautiful. Would you mind if I had a full tour sometime?"

That oddly nervous expression returned. "I'm the listing agent for the inn. I'd be happy to show you around."

Her words said one thing, but Randi's body language said something different. Maybe there was something wrong with the inn that she didn't want to reveal. But he knew she would have to before it could be sold. Maybe that information was saved for serious buyers, and he certainly didn't fit that description.

Right now, he'd push tonight's events out of his head, go back to the motel, and start working on moving his story to a small town like this one. And he'd figure out where in the book he could put the inn. Would it be a creepy, cobweb-littered inn or a polished one as he imagined it cleaned up and opened for business again?

CHAPTER EIGHT

Randi walked the motel's property as she did every morning. Well, every normal morning. Yesterday, she'd been grateful no one had needed anything—other than their water turned back on.

She picked up an empty soda can and noticed that the door on cottage 4 needed fresh paint. She stopped in the middle of the property. Actually, all the doors could use a fresh coat of paint. Maybe she'd go with shades of pink this time.

The men in town sometimes grumbled about the color, but they were adapting and saw the benefit of bringing more weddings to town. Not every bride or groom loved pink, but it immediately said *wedding* and seemed to clinch the deal for them to book their wedding in Two Hearts.

Cottage 5's guest and the mother-of-the-bride for tomorrow's wedding, Marguerite Watkins, waved Randi over to her door. Randi hoped there wasn't a problem that would require her to get her tools out. Or worse, something to do with the wedding. One wedding had been canceled at the last minute in April when the groom had decided he "needed to think it over." That had caused a cascade of problems, including an inconsolable bride.

The older woman dove into the conversation before Randi could greet her. "Did you know there are no open restaurants in the evening?"

Randi opened her mouth to reply.

"What am I supposed to do?" She glared at Randi as if she had personally set a policy that caused this.

"Dinah's Place has some dinner specials you can order in advance and put in your fridge."

The woman gave a single nod before closing the door.

Randi smiled. Problem solved. But she was glad she didn't have Cassie's job on Saturday as the wedding planner. But in the many years she'd been running her business, she'd probably seen it all.

When cottage 7's door opened, and John stepped out, Randi's heartbeat picked up. A response like that wasn't good. Hoping to just give a friendly wave as she passed him and scurry back to her office, she picked up her pace.

"Randi," John called out.

She stopped and turned to face him. When he stepped in front of her, she felt a flush spread over her body. *Rule One.* She took a deep breath and slowly let it out. "Can I help you with something, John?" That sounded suitably businesslike. Then she remembered the previous day. "There isn't a plumbing problem, is there?"

"Everything works fine."

Relief swept over her. "Thank goodness."

"I'm just enjoying my time in Two Hearts, so I've decided that I definitely want to stay longer. I hoped an opening at the motel had appeared so I could simply stay here."

She winced. "I'm sorry, but I can't add a single day. Some of the Saturday wedding party is already here, and the rest arrive later today and tomorrow. I could rent twice as many rooms if I had them." And she would once the inn was hers and open.

He stared at the ground then looked up. "Let's go with the rental option."

Randi's heart picked up in speed again. "Did you decide to stay permanently?"

John gave a lopsided grin. "After only a day in Two Hearts, I can't commit to that."

She realized how ridiculous her question sounded. Her heart had gotten her into this. Business would get her out. "I'm fairly certain no one will rent their house for a couple of days."

After a moment, he added, "I'll take it for the summer."

She blinked. *Months.* John would be here for months, but he's *still* not staying? She'd have to get her heart under control—and quickly. She couldn't avoid him for that long in a place this small.

She realized John was waiting for her to speak. "I could take you out to see possible rentals any time this afternoon. All the houses I'll show you are empty, so I don't have to make an appointment in advance. I'll need to make some calls before we go, though. These owners want to sell, so I have to confirm they'll rent."

"I just finished a chapter, so I'm at a great stopping point. I'm ready whenever you are."

"Give me fifteen minutes."

"Not enough time for another chapter, but I'll work on marketing. There's always something I can do for that."

Randi motioned with her arm toward her office. "I'll meet you over there. Oh, and my assumption is that you don't need anything too large."

"No, probably a two-bedroom house so I have a place to sleep and a separate workspace. I like to keep my office away from my living area so they're two separate parts of my life. Otherwise, I end up staring at my computer at all hours thinking I should work, and no one should work twenty-four hours a day."

Randi fought a sigh. Lately, it felt that way some days. She knew it would get better once the inn was hers. At least, she hoped it would. When she had the extra income from the inn, she'd be able to hire employees for her motel too. She just needed to have more guests to make everything work.

Right now, she was on her own. Some days, she felt that more than others.

When she sat at her desk, the to-do list for the inn caught her eye. Just this morning, she'd realized she could open the place up if only half of the rooms were finished. Then, she could fix up the other half during the off-season. Things had been a little quieter in January before weddings picked up again in the spring and summer, so that might work. Of course, she had to upgrade the plumbing, electric, and everything else in addition to fixing up the rooms.

She just had to hope that no one bought it before she could. A couple of calls had come in lately from people who could afford to outright purchase the property, but all indications were that they were only interested in the land. Yes, it would be a great place for a mansion on a lake, but not at the cost of the beautiful old building that was already there. So far, no one had asked her for more than a map of the land itself.

Today, her focus was on John and finding a house for him. Randi flipped through the files lined up in the drawer, one for every property listed through her. Each file folder included details and keys. She chose five she thought would work for John and called them. Only one turned her down for a short-term rental.

"Ready?" he asked when he opened the door to his cottage to her knock.

She dangled the keys for the first property. "I am. Are you serious about this?"

As soon as the words slipped out of her mouth, she wanted to pull them back. "I'm sorry. That's none of my business. I'm a real estate agent, and I represent my clients to the best of my ability."

He said, "No, I'm perfectly fine with that question. I know it seems sudden, but I had family that lived here a long time ago, and I'd like to spend some time in the town to explore my ancestry a little bit."

"Family?"

"Great-great-grandparents."

Family ties could make him choose to stay, but his ancestors were here a long time ago.

As they sat in the car on the way to the first property, Michelle's words from yesterday afternoon returned to her. This man was actually staying. Maybe *rule one* didn't apply anymore?

No. Randi pushed that thought out of her head because she had no idea about John's other commitments. He could have a fiancée somewhere waiting to join him. He'd need the same amount of room in a house for one person or two. And a short-term commitment was just that. Short term.

She'd focus on her job and be the best real estate agent she could be.

CHAPTER NINE

Randi followed John through the fourth house they'd been to this afternoon. After checking out every room, he returned to where they'd begun in the living room and stopped. He didn't seem to dislike anything, but he also didn't love it.

That wasn't necessarily critical for a rental because he wouldn't be staying long-term. But still, something seemed off.

"Not the one you want?"

He shook his head and walked over to the front window, looking out at the small lawn.

"I thought this would be easy." Randi immediately wanted to take back her words. That was rude for a real estate agent to say.

Instead of calling her out on it in a negative way, John said, "I did too. I thought I just wanted a place to sit and work. But now I wonder."

"Are you sure you want to stay in Two Hearts? Could that be the problem with your inability to commit?" She mentally added that these were four great houses that seemed to suit his purposes perfectly.

He spun around to face her with an excited expression on his face. "I think I figured it out. Are there any houses available to rent on the lake?"

"The lake?" She didn't even know he'd *seen* the lake. Both the inn and CJ and Paige's house were on the lake, but it had been pitch black when he'd been at both. She mentally went through her list of properties. "I have three that I can think of immediately. Those houses are all big Victorians. Two have five bedrooms and, if I'm not mistaken, the other one has six."

"Would any of them do a short-term rental?"

She pondered his question. "I'm pretty sure one of them will. I think I even made a note about that. It's possible one or more of the others will too. Let's go back to the office and get the keys. I definitely didn't bring one for any five-bedroom houses."

He chuckled. "I guess we'll call this the creative mind having its own way."

They went out the door and locked it behind them. "Okay, then let's see if a large house on the lake is the right place for you."

When they arrived at her motel office for the key, he followed her in.

"I'm just too antsy to sit. And I remember you had a wall map of Two Hearts."

"I do." She pointed to her right. "I got that not long ago."

He went over and studied it. "The lake's bigger than I realized. You can't see too much of it from the park. I went there this morning." He pointed at the map. "I guess this is the inn."

Randi glanced up from her search through the file drawer. "Looks about right. It's set back in a small bay." She sat down to examine the contents of the drawer more closely. "I thought it would be right here," she muttered. She knew it was one of two homes but wasn't sure which one.

John startled her when he leaned over the motel's front desk.

He'd crossed the room so silently she'd thought he was still by the map. "What's this?" He tapped her to-do list for the inn, the one where she listed everything she wanted to do once she'd bought it. She never should have left it out where someone might see it.

She decided to focus on what she was doing and pretend she hadn't heard him. Better to say nothing at all when it came to the inn. Fortunately, she came upon the right file. "Found it! I thought I'd made a note about renting for less than a year. It's the house to the left of CJ and Paige's when you're facing the lake."

He rubbed his hands together with glee. "Let's go see this place."

As they drove past the lake park, Randi realized there was something questionable about the house that she should probably mention. Hesitantly, she asked, "How do you feel about lavender?"

"The scent or the flower?"

She laughed. "Neither. The color."

"It's my mother's favorite. Why do you ask?"

"These big houses along here were painted lady Victorians. I suspect at one time, they were all done in pastel colors, but some of them were changed over the years." She slowed her car and motioned to her right. "This is where you were the other night—CJ and Paige's house. Paige bought it pink and repainted it that color when she fixed it up to keep the history. And this one," she stopped in front of the house next to it, "is the one I've brought you here to see."

Lavender paint covered the body of the house. The front door was a vibrant shade of yellow, and the trim was a crisp white. It always looked to her like an Easter basket.

She turned to him. "Are you ready?"

He grinned. "I'm ready."

A small yard with no front fence and an overgrown brick

walkway brought them from the street to a wide, covered front porch. As soon as they stepped in the door, John said, "This is it."

"Okay," Randi said slowly. "Can I ask why you think that when you went through the other houses from top to bottom and side to side and still didn't think they were right?"

"This one feels like home."

Randi knew what he meant. She had always thought that this house had a comfortable feel to it. Homey.

They stood in a central foyer with a parlor to the left and a dining room to the right. Just like CJ and Paige's house, the kitchen was straight back. "Before you make any sort of commitment, even for just a month or two, why don't you wander through the rest of the house to see what you think? Because some things need to be repaired."

She followed him into the kitchen. Cupboards from the 1950s or so covered two walls, forming an L, with a refrigerator and stove from the '70s or '80s inserted in between cupboards. A space in the corner next to a back door would be perfect for a kitchen table.

"Do the appliances work?"

"To the best of my knowledge, everything in the kitchen works. It's just dated."

He laughed. "It is that, but to me, it's a charming oldness. Though a fresh coat of cream paint on the cupboards and the walls would help."

"Go through there." She pointed to the right. "You'll find a butler's pantry. Keep going to the dining room."

He did as she instructed. "This room could hold a large dining room table." He continued through the foyer to the parlor, which had one overstuffed armchair with a navy and red floral-patterned fabric. "All of this looks good. And the tiles around the fireplace appear original, though I probably don't need a roaring fire in the summer."

"You definitely don't in Tennessee. The chair in the corner looks comfy."

He sat down. "It is. This is the only furniture I've seen. Is there any upstairs?"

"Bedrooms and bathrooms are upstairs. There's some scattered furniture."

"More than one bathroom? I'll probably have family visiting at some point."

She waved her hand from side to side. "Sort of."

"How do you have sort of a bathroom?"

"A toilet kept running, and the owner didn't want to pay to fix it. We turned it off."

"That's it—just running?"

She nodded.

"I can certainly fix that."

"The rent in Two Hearts is on the low side, so I don't know if the owners are going to reimburse you for any repairs." She quoted him the price the owner wanted per month.

He brushed the comment aside. "It's so inexpensive that it doesn't matter. And it'll give me something to do when I'm not writing."

They went up threadbare carpet-covered stairs to the upper story, which had wood floors. "The main bedroom is over here."

John walked into a bedroom that could easily hold a king-sized bed and had an attached bathroom. "This was a luxury in its day."

Randi said, "I think that was added at some point after the house was built."

The room next door had a bed and dresser. "Is this an old bed I wouldn't want to use?"

"It's almost new. The owner was aging and started needing help, so her grandson moved in to assist her. He ordered the bed and settled in, but only for two or three weeks. After making the drive to Nashville and back every weekday—ninety minutes each way when it's just light traffic—he talked her into moving to the apartment next door to him. The house has been empty since then."

Another room had a large, antique rolltop desk. John rubbed his hand across the surface. "Beautiful old wood." When he tried the rolltop on the desk itself, it slid beautifully, revealing a desk that he'd be happy to use. The wooden chair on wheels that went with the desk was a fun addition. "I'm going to enjoy working here." After crossing the room to the large window, he added, "I'll have a view of the lake, which means I may not get as much work done, but I don't think I care." He grinned.

They finally arrived at the second bathroom. John went in, got on the floor to inspect the plumbing, and stood. "Okay, this all looks fine to me. Where do I sign?"

"You're sure?"

"Positive. I can see myself living here."

"Do you want to tour the attic? I've been up there, and there are supplies you could use for repairs."

"I can check it out later."

She wasn't sure why she was pushing him for confirmation. He sounded like he knew exactly what he was doing. "I have a rental agreement. I'll have to send it over to the owner for him to sign, of course, but I should be able to get back to you today. Tomorrow at the latest."

As they went down the stairs, John asked, "How long did you say I have in the motel room before I'm kicked to the curb?"

Randi laughed. "I'd rather you worded it *gently asked to leave.* I need a Friday checkout, so you have until tomorrow at 11:00 a.m. I'd love to extend that, but I have to clean before new guests check in, and I'll have the rest of the wedding party checking in midday."

"I have a bed, a chair, and a desk here. That should work out perfectly." He seemed to be hesitating about something. She hoped he hadn't changed his mind about the rental. "I feel like I owe my real estate agent something for finding me the perfect place. And for not being too upset with me when I passed up others that were all equally perfect on paper."

Smiling, she said, "Or more perfect since they had the number of bedrooms you requested and not so many that your whole family could visit."

"I haven't had anywhere big enough for my parents, sister, and brother to visit in a long time. I didn't know I wanted that option, but it turns out that I do."

Since he hadn't at any point mentioned a significant other in his life, Randi decided he must be single. Her foolish heart pitter-pattered at the thought.

"You're okay with lavender?" As soon as she said the words, she wanted to snatch them back instead of emphasizing the paint color issue.

John laughed. "Remember, it's my mother's favorite color. She liberally used lavender in our home. My dad is a rough-and-tumble football coach, but he didn't mind, so I can live with it. And it's only outside. I didn't notice a single pastel color inside the house."

"It'll make your mom happy if she comes to visit."

He grinned. "It definitely will. Where do I sign?"

Randi sorted through the folders in the bag at her side, pulling out the one with the rental forms. As she opened the folder, John reached for the blank contract on top, and their hands brushed against each other. An electric charge shot up her arm—just like in the romance novels she'd read.

Randi jerked her hand back then rubbed her still-tingling hand on her pant leg. Taking a deep breath, she focused on her job. As casually as she could manage, she closed the folder and tucked it back in her bag, hoping John hadn't noticed anything amiss.

When she looked up, John was staring at her with an odd expression.

"Are you all right?" she asked.

He blinked a couple of times and then looked down at the paper in his hand as though he was seeing it for the first time. "Yes. Fine. Absolutely." He nodded. "I took this from you, but you must need to add information because it's all blank."

"I do."

Those words immediately reminded her of a wedding, but she pushed away visions of her in white walking down an aisle. John handed the pages back, and she carefully took them from him so they wouldn't touch. Then she entered the details—his name, the property's address, the length of term, the monthly rent, and other information.

She started for the kitchen, saying, "We need a surface for you to sign on." She placed the document on the kitchen counter. "If the details work for you, then all you need to do is sign here." She pointed. "And initial here."

He read through the two-page document. "So it's for two months with an option for another two months?"

"I think that's what you wanted, right? Two months to start with?"

"That's correct. But why two months more?"

"I wanted to make sure you could extend it if you wanted to stay longer. I always add terms like that to a rental contract."

He shrugged. "Makes sense. Do you think they'd mind, though, if I changed the number to six months?"

That caught her off guard. "*Six* months?" He kept telling her he hadn't decided about staying in Two Hearts, but then he did things like that.

"I like it here and want to see how that evolves. I may decide I don't have any emotional connection to the town, but if I want to stay here, I would like to have that option."

Giddiness rose up in her chest. She knew she shouldn't get excited about the possibility of him staying because it was still very much a maybe, but she couldn't help herself. Her friend's words of caution kept reminding her to be careful, but a man who was considering staying for more than half a year may be okay to fall for. At least a little bit.

John signed the documents and slid the pages over to her, seeming to do that as carefully as she had. Randi was grateful for his caution. But then again, she wasn't. Michelle's *rule one* was not going well.

The only option to completely protect her heart was to keep her distance from John. Falling into the trap of hoping he'd stay, pretending everything was okay, left her wide open for disaster when he decided Two Hearts wasn't for him.

Randi had to give John a wide berth. She was so busy right now that she shouldn't have a problem doing that.

CHAPTER TEN

The owner of the house John wanted to rent—the grandson of the woman who'd last lived here—was giddy about earning money instead of only paying out. Randi had called with the proposed terms and emailed him the contract. Instead of taking time to contemplate the short-term rental offer as she'd expected he would, he'd signed and returned it within minutes.

John moved out of her motel and into his house early Friday morning. She cleaned his room and two others, then checked in the bridal party and guests.

Once that was done, she released Jasper from his fenced run and took him for a walk.

"Are you ready for a busy day, boy?" His woof in reply told her he understood and was ready for the job. Especially if the job included a long walk with a possible treat when they arrived back home.

Randi took a route up Main Street, past the shops and Dinah's to the lake. Unless her phone rang with an emergency, she had a break until a real estate client's scheduled home tour in a couple of hours.

There's no way that she'd chosen this route in case she just happened to run into John. That would make her like a teenage girl wanting to see her crush.

That definitely wasn't her.

When his vehicle wasn't at the curb in front of his house, and he wasn't outside, she told herself it didn't matter anyway. They were taking a walk, and there were only so many routes you could choose when you were in a small town. It was pure coincidence.

And he was still in Two Hearts temporarily. Sure, he had a family connection to the town, but lots of people had family who'd lived in other places. They didn't move there.

Back at the motel, Jasper received his expected treat and settled onto his bed beside her desk when she sat down. This had been one of the mornings that she'd come to look forward to and dread at the same time. New customers brought new life and income to her motel, but the turnover and cleaning brought a lot more work—most of it all at once.

Her motel was currently fully booked and at the higher wedding rate. Each room had a special gift basket with snacks, toiletries, and the brochure about the town that Amy from the newspaper had put together and printed. The small fridges were stocked with snacks and drinks. Regular guests didn't seem interested enough in those perks to pay extra, but bridal guests wanted special treatment.

Randi leaned back in her chair, picturing her life once she had someone to clean her motel and run the front desk. Of course, the only way she could see that happening was if she had more units to rent, which meant she needed the inn.

"Soon." She sighed because she'd scheduled tonight for work on room 214 at the inn. More cleaning, and if there was time, she'd start painting the walls." The inn, combined with her usual motel work, made for a busy life.

Right now, she just needed to close her eyes for a few

minutes. Sounds in the distance had her open one eye. *Why was someone in her bedroom?*

A woman was walking toward her. Randi jumped. Then she realized she was in the motel's office.

The woman eyed her. "Sorry to bother you, but could I get a couple more towels?"

At that moment, the motel's phone rang.

Maybe she'd clean that room another night.

After the guest left, Randi got a cup of coffee, inhaled it, and then began organizing her files for the day by removing everything from the previous day from her tote bag. She pulled out those from John's house hunt and tossed them on her desk. When she opened the one he'd rented to make a copy of the rental agreement for him to keep, two keys on a small key ring were tacked inside.

Randi blew out a breath. She'd only given him the key to the front door. Once he'd touched her hand, she'd forgotten everything, including her name. She pulled the keys off the folder and checked them. One was labeled for the back door and the other for the shed. He might be able to get by without a key to the back door, but she knew a lawn mower was in that shed, along with some outdoor furniture he would probably like to use.

She'd decided to keep her distance, but now she had no choice.

Randi slipped the keys into a pocket on the side of her bag. Unless she asked someone else to deliver them, she had to see John today. She definitely couldn't leave the key to unlock the door to the man's house on his front step. She needed to hand it to him personally.

But she wouldn't stay. She'd drop the keys in his hand—without touching—and be on her way.

~

Randi hesitated with her hand over the door as she prepared to knock. *You're the real estate agent. You have every reason to be here. This is not a romantic gesture. You're just delivering keys to a client who rented a home through you. That's it.*

She knocked firmly and stood with her shoulders back. She would give John the keys, turn around, and leave. Easy peasy.

"Remember the *first rule*. Never date anyone who isn't planning to stay here. *First rule.* Deep breath. *First rule.*"

The door opened, and she looked up into Mrs. Brantley's face.

"What are you saying, dear? Something about rules?"

Randi blinked a few times as she stared at the older woman. "Is John Morgan here?"

"Have you come to see him?" she asked with a little too much glee.

"I rented the house to him, and I forgot to give him a couple of the keys."

"Who's there?" John asked from a distance.

When she gave her name, John said, "Come on back."

Mrs. Brantley gave her a wink and stepped out. "Enjoy your evening."

And now it would be all over town that she was dating John. Life as a real estate agent sometimes meant she was in situations like this, but a young single woman alone with a young single man inevitably led to rumors. It might not bother her if she was actually dating the man gossip said she was.

Shaking her head, Randi went inside and was about to ask where he was when heavenly scents assailed her. Sounds from the kitchen confirmed John's location. She came around the corner to find him at the stove, stirring one pan as he took the lid off another to check on its contents.

Four cardboard boxes were off to the side of the room, one of them open with linens peeking out. John must have started unpacking whatever he'd brought.

"I'm sorry I couldn't come to the door, but my sauce may burn if I walk away for even a minute at this stage."

"No problem." What other response was there when a man's sauce was about to burn? "You definitely know how to cook, don't you? This wasn't something Mrs. Brantley just dropped off."

He looked over his shoulder at her with a grin. "No. The mayor came by to introduce herself. Apparently, the sheriff told her I was a new resident."

"Have you met Greg?"

"The first day I was here. He shared a table with me. Or rather, I shared a table with him at the diner right before you joined me."

"Greg's last name is Brantley. That's his mother."

John softly laughed, a warm sound that tried to wrap its way around her heart.

"That makes sense. She probably knows what's going on from him."

"Oh, that's sometimes a shorter route for her to acquire information, but believe me, Emmaline Brantley knows everything that's going on in town almost before the people involved do."

"Since I have nothing to hide, I'm fine."

She needed to adopt that attitude. Then she remembered the inn and her own secrets and realized caution was best.

John motioned to his right. "Would you put the biscuits in the oven? I cut them out but had to take care of this."

"I'm sure I can do that. But don't ask me to make them from scratch." She went to the kitchen counter beside the stove. A floured surface had a dozen biscuits cut out, with a cookie sheet right beside them.

"You can find something to lift them with in here." He tapped the kitchen drawer in front of her. "You don't enjoy cooking?"

Randi used a spatula to lift a biscuit onto the tray. "That's a great question." She continued her project as she thought about it. "I don't dislike cooking, but, to me, cooking is more because I need to and not because I think it's fun." She turned to face him with the baking tray in her hands. "Done."

"Thanks." He took the tray from her and slid it in the oven. Then he held up a spoonful of sauce. "Is the seasoning in this cheese sauce right?"

Randi tasted it, and the creamy flavor rolled over her tongue. "Oh, my! So good." She leaned over to see what else he was cooking.

"I have a roast chicken in the oven, the cheese sauce to go over some cauliflower— because that's my favorite way to eat it —and pasta with homemade pesto." John reached for the kitchen drawer as she straightened, which brought his arm around her waist and her face near his.

She looked into his eyes, and her gaze dropped to his mouth. All thoughts flew out of her head except the one about how she really wanted to kiss him.

John slowly leaned toward her, his breath warm against her face.

He brushed his hand over her cheek. "Flour," he said, leaving his hand there.

She knew she should step away. Her heartbeat pounded, drowning her thoughts.

Move away, Randi.

Rule one flew out the window as John moved closer. Her eyes fluttered closed.

Buzzzzzz.

John jumped away from her. "That's, uh, the timer's alarm." He turned off a burner. "The pasta's ready."

"Of course." Her heart still racing, Randi went to the kitchen window, looking out but barely noticing anything there. She needed to remember why she was in his house. This shouldn't be a casual conversation where she got to know him better. She had to turn it back to business.

"I'm here because I neglected to give you two of the keys for the property." That was suitably official, wasn't it? "For the back door and the shed."

"Excellent." John's voice sounded strained. He cleared his throat before adding, "I was wondering about that shed because I'm hoping there's a mower in there. It's going to take quite a bit of work to have this field of weeds look anything like a lawn again." He drained the pasta in the sink.

"If you're going to work on the property while you're here and make any improvements, I'm pretty sure we can get you a discount on your rent."

"That's okay. I would feel guilty paying less. I'm in a beautiful old house on a lake for a quarter of the rent I paid in Florida for a one-bedroom apartment with a so-so view. I'm living like royalty in comparison."

"Let me know if you change your mind. It'll definitely help the owner sell the house if it's more inviting." She just wished the inn's owner was interested in improvements. He just wanted someone to write him a check. "Well, I'd better be going."

"Would you like to stay and have dinner?"

His words were simple, but she couldn't let herself be pulled in. After that almost-kiss, spending time alone with John was the last thing she should do. "Thank you, but no. I'm not ready for dinner yet."

At that exact moment, her stomach did the cliché thing and rumbled probably louder than it had in her entire life. That's what she got for trying to live on just a snack bar for lunch. Her traitorous stomach had experienced the cheese sauce and wanted more.

John laughed. "The plates are in the cupboard. I've rewashed everything because even though things were closed up, they all had a layer of dust on them. And the silverware's in that drawer." He pointed to the drawer under that cupboard.

Randi tried to come up with a reasonable excuse for leaving, but everything that came to mind would sound rude. Besides, it couldn't hurt to have dinner here. She pulled silverware out of the drawer then stood looking around. "John, did you buy a table? I didn't notice one when I came in."

He turned to her and winced. "That's on my list of things to do. Yesterday and today, I ate while sitting on that chair in the parlor. I guess I was so excited about having you here—I mean company—that I forgot."

At this point, Randi knew she would stay for dinner, even if it had just been a sandwich and chips. An open cardboard box with blankets and towels peeking out the top gave her an idea. "What about a picnic? Maybe here on the kitchen floor. Or we could make the meal more formal and sit on the dining room floor."

John grinned. "I'll let you choose."

Randi spread the blanket on the floor in the corner of the room. "I would ask what you've been doing this afternoon, but it looks like you've been cooking."

"I'm happy to say I got in the writing I needed to, and my story is coming along nicely. I was setting it at a big house on the Gulf Coast, so it was fairly easy to move it to a lake. The male main character was dismayed to find that his rental was painted lavender."

Randi grinned. "It is rather a shock to the senses, isn't it?"

"Yes. But I also had time to send my mom a photo of the house and call her. She's pretty excited about the color. Even better than that, I'm only a few hours from them now, so she and Dad are already planning a visit for next month."

He put the food into serving bowls and the chicken on a platter, then handed each to her to add to their makeshift picnic space. The two of them sat down, John cross-legged and Randi with her legs to the side.

As they ate, the conversation became more relaxed and comfortable. He was easy to be around. "If anything, this food tastes better than it smelled. If you'd asked me earlier, I would have thought that was impossible."

"Thank you. It's nice to cook for someone." He spread butter on a biscuit then topped it with strawberry jam.

She wondered if he meant someone special or just another human being. Dwelling on thoughts like that wouldn't get her anywhere. She asked, "Do you usually switch your books to different places or make changes like the setting in the middle of writing one?"

"Not often, but writing is so much about what feels right to me, and I'm not strict about an outline. Nothing is set in concrete before I start writing. The story evolves and shifts as the book comes together. I started writing it in Florida, so that setting made perfect sense to me, but continuing like that didn't feel right once I was here. I'll probably add other things about this house or Two Hearts in the story, maybe without even meaning to."

"Have you found anything that's an unwelcome surprise since you moved in?"

"Everything is as you said it would be. I drove to the town with the pizza place and got the part I needed to fix the toilet. It works perfectly now."

"You really can fix things."

He turned toward her and grinned.

"But you didn't have to go that far for a hardware store. We have one here in town."

"Seriously? I thought I'd driven most of the roads here and never saw one."

"One street over from Main Street. Anybody can tell you

how to get there. And if Sam doesn't already have what you need, he can usually get a part in in a day or two."

By the time she'd finished the meal, they had laughed often, and she had thoroughly enjoyed herself.

"Thank you for staying. There's no one I'd rather have a picnic with." Then he added, "I'm enjoying my visit to Two Hearts."

Visit. Michelle was absolutely right. While Michelle may have struck gold when she found a man who was willing to live here permanently for her, that probably wouldn't happen twice.

"Well." Randi stood. "I appreciate the dinner. It was the best thing I've eaten in a long time, but don't you dare tell Dinah. I have paperwork to do and a couple of small projects to complete, so I'd better go. Not to mention, I need to stop and pick Jasper up from Michelle's. He likes to hang out in their backyard and play with the goats. He met them when he was a puppy and seems to see them as dogs." She laughed.

"You can drop him off here sometime. I checked the backyard to see what was out there. It's fully fenced and secure. I'm happy to have him run around while I work. When I take a break, I could throw a stick for him."

She stopped in her tracks. That felt a little too ... cozy. But she liked to do what she could to make Jasper happy. He ended up stuck inside or in his small, fenced run more than she wanted. And he definitely liked John.

"I may take you up on that."

"Please do. And I enjoy cooking, so I'll be here most nights. Feel free to drop by and join me again." John's smile began melting the walls she'd put around her heart, so she hurried toward the door, hoping for grace and dignity as she made her escape. Both vanished when her pant leg caught the edge of a box, and she hurtled toward the wood floor.

John grabbed her and tugged her in close to hold her upright.

The doorbell rang.

They sprang apart.

Saved by the bell. *Again.*

He frowned. "I need to see who that is."

Neither one of them moved.

"Yes, good idea."

John sighed when the bell rang again. "Would you like to join me for dinner tomorrow? We could go formal." He nudged his head in the direction of the dining room.

Her mind urged her to say Yes*!* But she knew she had to tell him no. "I'm sorry, but I can't."

He went toward the door, with Randi following him, dazed. That had been a close call. Literally saved by the bell.

Greg and Micah were outside on the porch.

Greg said, "We were driving by, and I told Micah you'd moved in. We wanted to let you know if you needed any help with the yard, we'd be happy to help."

"A bunch of the guys helped clear out the brush next door. We're experienced now," Micah added.

Then Greg saw her behind him.

"Oh, I'm sorry, I didn't know that you had company."

Both men grinned.

Randi stepped around John. In what she hoped was her usual business tone of voice, she said, "I needed to drop off some keys for the property and happened upon John when he was almost ready to eat, so he invited me to stay. I tell you, Nick may be a professional Nashville chef, but he's going to have a run for his money with the cooking among the men in this town. The meal was delicious." She extended her hand to John, and he shook it, the gleam in his eyes telling her he knew what she was trying to do. "Thank you so much, John. I appreciated it."

She stepped out the door and around the men, not hearing a word of their conversation as she walked away but hearing laughter when she was almost to her car. She was glad she'd kept her dignity intact.

But at the same time, she wished that doorbell hadn't rung. Maybe the almost kiss would have become real.

CHAPTER ELEVEN

Two days after Randi's visit, John answered a knock on his door, hoping it would be her. He hadn't seen her since then, and in a town this size, that seemed odd.

Instead of a thirtyish woman, he found the mayor and a much older man leaning on a cane who, in comparison, made the sixty-something Mrs. Brantley look young enough to be a teenager.

He couldn't imagine why they'd be paying him a visit. "Can I help you?"

"Actually," the mayor said, "I think we have excellent news for you. She patted the man on his shoulder. "This is Carlton Trimble, our town's historian."

The older man smiled. "Not so much as a profession. The title grew with me over time because I'd lived long enough to remember more of the history than anyone else does." He gave a low, rumbling chuckle.

"Well, please come in." John stood back so the man could hobble in.

Mr. Trimble went straight for the sitting room—at a slow but steady pace, so John and Mrs. Brantley followed.

"Can I get you something to drink? I have sweet tea I just made. I'm trying to learn the ways of the South."

Mr. Trimble folded himself onto the sofa so slowly that John wondered if they'd ever raise him up again. "That would be delightful, young man."

John returned a few minutes later, his curiosity growing by the second as to why they had come here.

Mr. Trimble leaned forward, his expression serious. "It's my understanding that your family has long roots in this town, in the inn specifically. Is that correct?"

When a historian asked him a question like that, it raised all kinds of red flags in John's mind. Had his family done something worthy of note? Perhaps criminal? "Is there something wrong I should know about?" John asked cautiously, realizing as he spoke that Mr. Trimble had probably uncovered the story about the poker game causing the loss of the inn.

"Oh, my, no. At least, nothing I'm aware of. However, this is something I think will please you greatly. You see, this house was owned by the people who built the inn, by your ancestors. That's why it's next door to the inn. They built this house first and stayed here while the inn was being constructed. Then, they lived here while they operated the inn. It's my understanding that there used to be a stone pathway between the two properties."

He waved toward the direction of the side yard. "My guess is that it's still in that mess of brush and trees."

John leaned back in his chair, dumbfounded.

"So my ancestors lived *here*?" He opened his hands wide to gesture toward the room around them. "In this building? Not another building on this site—but in this very dwelling?"

"Yes, sir. This is the only house to have been built here, to my knowledge. And it goes back to the days of the inn. Predates it, actually, by a short time."

"Wow." John felt a grin start and spread so wide that it hurt his cheeks. "That is fantastic. I came here to find family history."

"And you ended up sleeping in it. Wonderful."

"Is there anything else you can tell me about the place?"

"Only that the house wasn't this color. When I found an old newspaper article about it, it said it was a soft yellow color with olive trim and ochre window frames."

"So changing it from lilac to those colors would be making it historically correct, and that should make everyone happy."

Mr. Trimble gave a toothy grin. "Especially the gentlemen in this town, I suspect."

Could this day get any better? The older man nudged himself forward on the couch, came to a partial stand while bent over his cane, and then straightened. More or less.

"Thank you very much for coming here today. Both of you."

Mrs. Brantley patted him on the arm. "You're welcome. We're glad to have you in our town."

Mr. Trimble said, "I enjoy history, but I know the town needs to survive to make new history. Too many people have left, so everyone is happy when someone new moves in."

"Some, perhaps, more than others." She gave him a smile.

He had no doubt she was referring to Randi. But at this point, he had no idea where that was going, if it was going anywhere.

After they had left, he returned to the room and sat down. The fireplace across from him had what he knew must be original tile. His great-great-grandmother had likely chosen it.

He was still determined to do a lot of work in the kitchen because, except possibly one cabinet, nothing in there appeared to have Victorian origins. Kitchens didn't have modern cupboards on all walls in those days. They had used separate pieces of furniture.

Maybe this winter, when all the brush had died back, he'd be able to find that path through the woods to the inn. His ties to the inn and the town felt stronger now than they ever had.

As much as he wanted to continue on his planned trip, Two Hearts was becoming home. Should he make the decision to buy this house now that he knew it had belonged to his ancestors? He couldn't imagine walking away from this house when he already felt comfortable living there. He wouldn't want the complications of owning the inn, so this could be the piece of his family history that he kept.

And then there was Randi. She was a special part of Two Hearts.

He hadn't considered it when he'd rented, so he hadn't asked about the purchase price. Knowing the condition it was in and the lack of maintenance on basics such as the toilet, he suspected it wasn't too steep.

John went outside, walked to the middle of his front yard, and looked up at the house. *My great-great-grandparents lived* here. Of course, they had to leave in disgrace when his great-great-grandfather lost the inn.

But maybe selling the house was what helped them move elsewhere. He'd have to dig into old records to see what he could find.

Now, he really wanted to tell someone about this. His parents had never had any interest in the stories, but his grandfather did. John took out his phone and tapped Grandpa's number. When the call went to voicemail, he realized this was Tuesday afternoon, and that meant he was playing golf with his buddies.

As he hung up, he saw Randi's car drive by. It was early afternoon, long before she usually went to the inn, but that must be her destination. From what he'd seen, there wasn't much down the road past the inn other than a few neglected properties that made the abandoned inn look new in comparison.

He headed down his walk through the gate and down the road. With every step, he realized more and more that in the short time he'd known her, Randi had become important to him. He didn't want to tell just anyone his news—he wanted to share his exciting news with Randi.

That wasn't good because she hadn't encouraged him in any way. Any time he caught a whiff of possible interest, he realized he was wrong. They had a professional relationship through real estate—and possibly a new friendship.

He picked up his pace. Friends share good news with friends, right?

When he got to the long drive at the inn and started up, he soon saw her little silver car parked there, and his heart rate kicked up. He had almost kissed her, and she hadn't stopped him.

"Morgan, you have got it bad. How did this slip up on you without your noticing?"

Then he realized he *had* noticed, but he'd kept pushing it to the side.

He assumed she'd already gone inside, so he was surprised when her car door opened, and Jasper shot out and raced over to him. "Ouch! Please wait until Mom gets out."

Jasper danced around John's feet with his tail wagging so hard it shook his whole hind end.

"How are you? Are you being a good boy?" John scratched the dog behind his ears.

Randi got out and looked at John, and her smile lit up her face in a way that told him she had to have some interest in him. At least, he hoped she did.

He took a few more steps before sharing his good news with her.

"My great-great-grandparents built the house I rented."

Randi clipped a leash on her dog, who stayed beside John.

"Amazing." She shook her head. "That's the one that felt right when you stepped inside. You'll have to take pictures so you can remember it after you've left."

At that moment, he realized he'd known Two Hearts was home from the day he'd arrived. This wasn't a short-term visit. "You said the owners were willing to rent, but they're also willing to sell, correct?"

Randi's expression became more businesslike. "Absolutely. Any house I'm renting can be purchased. They're resorting to renting as a way to keep up with basic maintenance and expenses."

"I may want to buy it."

She blinked several times. "What did you say?"

"I have to think about it a little longer, but I think I want to buy the house I'm living in." The more he thought about it, the more the idea appealed to him.

"You're staying in Two Hearts?"

"I think I am."

Her face lit up again. "That's great news!" She threw her arms around him and hugged him. Then she stepped back, clasping her hands in front of herself. "Sorry. That wasn't professional. What I should say is that I'll draw up the paperwork for you. We can talk about the purchase price tomorrow."

John reached for Randi, wrapped his arms around her, and swung her around in the air. He focused his gaze on her face for a moment, then lowered his mouth toward hers, gently touching his lips to hers, giving her a chance to step away. When she leaned into him, he deepened the kiss.

She stepped back a moment later and put her hand on her mouth. In a quiet voice, she said, "That's the first time a real estate client has kissed me."

His mistake hit him. He had crossed a line and must have misread the signals. "I'm sorry. I was out of line."

Her brow furrowed. "No, that's—"

He cut in to help her out. "I know you're my real estate agent, and that was inappropriate. Please forget it ever happened."

He pulled his gaze from her. His chest ached because he'd gotten this so wrong. "I'm sorry." Then he turned and walked away.

When John reached the end of the driveway, he realized he was all but jogging home, so he slowed his steps. What had he done? That kiss was a mistake—or was it?

Once home, he didn't go inside. He sat on his front step and looked over his still mostly wild yard. He'd pulled a few weeds, but that was it.

He'd wanted to share his news with the woman he was growing to care about but had gotten ahead of himself. She seemed to like him as a person. But she clearly saw him as just a real estate client.

Did he still want the house? He'd have to work with Randi and see her around town.

Yes. What had just happened hadn't changed his interest in the town.

But that brought up the memory of their kiss. He hoped he hadn't ruined what they had because kissing Randi was something he wanted to repeat, not forget. He'd have to take it slower.

CHAPTER TWELVE

As Randi waited for her friend Michelle to arrive for what she'd called an emergency dinner in her earlier text to her, Randi went over for what must be the hundredth time what had happened earlier today.

When she'd gone through it the first time—while John was walking down the driveway and away from her—she'd realized her mistake.

Her words had come back to her. *This is the first time a real estate client has kissed me.* That had been stupid, stupid, stupid. John thought he'd crossed the line with someone who only wanted a business relationship.

Even Jasper had known something was wrong because he'd barked when John moved out of sight at the end of the driveway.

"You're right, boy. I made a mistake. We need to find a way to tell John the truth."

She touched her fingers to her lips as she remembered what had happened. The moment now felt like a dream. No longer interested in working on the inn, she'd loaded her dog back into the car and headed toward home.

A knock on her door brought Randi back to the present. She opened her door to Michelle. "I'm glad you could come." Then she realized what had probably been a mistake. "Wait! Did you leave your husband alone at home?" She kept forgetting her friend had gotten married.

"Sam left for what he promised would be a quick trip. I have leftover chicken and dumplings and chocolate pie from Dinah's."

"Bring it over here!" Randi gestured toward the small, round table in what she called her dining room, but was really just a corner of a square room that included her tiny kitchen and a living room big enough for a couch and not much else. "You're the best guest because you bring the food."

Both of them laughed.

After they'd eaten, Michelle pushed her plate to the side. "Now, give." She motioned forward with her hands. "You said this was an emergency."

Randi's heart rate picked up as it usually did when she thought about John. "I thought he was only going to stay a few days, then a month, and now he says he's moving here."

Her friend's brow furrowed. "He? I think I missed the beginning of the story."

Randi thought about how quickly everything had moved. She hadn't had time to talk to Michelle in a few days. Besides, her friend's husband had been in town, and she tried to give the newlyweds time alone when he'd been away traveling for a couple of weeks.

"The guest. John Morgan. The one who helped me with the plumbing."

Michelle stared at her with an incredulous expression. "The one I pushed you toward for the downtown tour?"

"That's the one. He rented the house next to CJ and Paige. He told me yesterday he may want to buy it."

"Which side? The lavender house or the brown one?"

"Lavender. It turns out that his great-great-grandparents owned it. *Rule One* keeps coming to mind."

"If he's staying, my rule doesn't apply."

"Michelle, he keeps talking about all of the places he's lived. And he said he *might* want to buy it. I wouldn't be surprised if he fixed up the house and rented it out. You know that something in good shape on the lake could probably be rented now."

Michelle blew out a breath. "He hasn't been here long, so just stay away. You couldn't have fallen for him already."

Randi felt tears welling in her eyes.

Without missing a beat, Michelle sighed. "You fell for him? Does he know?"

"He kissed me!" she blurted out.

Her friend grinned. "I don't see the problem."

"Then he apologized."

"Okay. That's awkward. Is there something you aren't telling me? Because I'm not seeing much of a problem."

"You might be right. I could just be tired." Randi closed her eyes, and it felt good to rest for even a few seconds. Maybe she just needed time off.

"That makes more sense. Next time you see John, show him somehow that you're interested."

Nothing made things clearer for her than talking to a friend. "I'll do that." She desperately needed some fun. "Are you ready for pie? And then a movie?"

Michelle laughed. "After handing out slices of pie all day, you'd think it would be the last thing I'd want, but I've never lost my love of Dinah's pies." She pulled the bag with dessert in it toward them. "Then I'm in for a movie. Rom-com?"

Randi winced. "Maybe something with adventure. I don't think I'm in the mood for a romance."

Michelle shrugged. "You might get tips."

Randi pushed on her friend's arm and laughed, feeling better already. "No thank you."

"Then adventure it is."

CHAPTER THIRTEEN

Randi rushed from her car toward the inn's entrance, Jasper moving ahead of her. When she burst out of the vines and brush into the small clearing near the door, she leaned her head back to check the sky. Dark clouds skittered by. "We'd better get to work and leave earlier than normal tonight to beat the worst of the coming storm."

Her dog woofed in agreement.

As they headed toward the front door, a gust of wind hurried them along. "Jasper, what are we going to do about this situation with John?"

The dog didn't make a sound, so he apparently had no comment on the situation. And this was a dog that wasn't afraid to let her know what he thought.

She tried to come every day or at least every other day. But John had kissed her two days ago, and then she'd had her girls' night with Michelle. Yesterday, she'd had a busy from-morning-till-night day at the motel. Randi wanted to—*needed* to—make forward progress on this place. Fixing up this place as much as she could before she bought it would speed up her opening once she'd signed the papers and made this place hers.

Upstairs, she got to work cleaning a new guestroom. After moving the dresser and nightstands to where they should be, she dusted the outside of the wood-burning fireplace then began cleaning the ashes that had been left inside. Every time she did this, she was surprised by the beauty that appeared when the dirt came off.

Some rooms, like this one, still had drapes and a fully made bed with sheets and a coverlet. Next time she came—on a day without a storm, she'd take down the drapes and shake them outside to remove the dust. Tonight, she continued her cleaning by sweeping cobwebs from corners then dusting and polishing the wood furniture.

Low rumbles of thunder in the distance preceded winds that rattled the old building.

Jasper was becoming more and more agitated. The howling wind had him howling back.

"Hush, boy. It's going to be okay." He nuzzled against her leg, and she rubbed the side of his head. "Don't worry." That calmed him a little for now, but he still seemed agitated.

Lightning brightened the room then thunder sounded. As the weather turned worse outside, Randi realized she'd better cut her work short. This storm was stronger than she'd expected. She put the cleaning supplies back on the old cart she'd found in the housekeeping closet and wheeled it to the side of the room where she'd leave it until she continued her work here.

The sky opened up, and rain pelted the window. If this place had electricity on, it would probably have flickered a time or two by now. As it was, the storm had darkened the sky, making it seem later than it was. Randi turned on her phone's flashlight app.

Branches of a tree brushed against the side of the building— one of the top items on her list of things that must immediately be taken care of if she bought this inn. No, she corrected herself.

When she bought the inn. Trees and branches that threatened the building had to be removed. So many had gotten out of control.

Another gust hit, the branches smacking the side of the building and the window, not just giving a gentle brush like before. The night reminded her of an old gothic novel. Darkness, rain, wind … and she was all alone in an isolated location. Randi wrapped her arms across her chest.

They needed to leave here now.

Jasper howled, which was the last thing she needed in the middle of a situation like this.

"Don't worry."

Her dog howled again as he stared at the window, which suddenly shattered before Randi's eyes. She screamed and jumped back, grabbing Jasper as she did to pull both of them away from the broken glass.

But that wasn't even the worst of it because an open window in a storm would cause damage she'd later have to repair.

"I need a tarp. A board. Something! *Think*, Randi." Nothing she had here or in her car would work, and the hardware store was closed.

She grabbed her phone and called CJ, who must have at least one board on hand. When his phone went to voicemail, she remembered he'd gotten tickets for a concert in Nashville and taken Paige for the night. He knew how much she loved music, so he did that every few months.

But who else would have what she needed? The wind was blowing the rain in the opposite direction, but any second now, it could shift and push a torrent of rain directly into this room.

John was next door, and she was sure she had seen stuff like this piled up in his attic. She had managed to avoid talking to him since what she'd come to think of as *The Kiss*. Even with Michelle's advice, or maybe because of it, she hadn't yet figured out what to say and how to act.

Randi pulled out her phone and debated her call. A gust of wind blew the drapes into a dancing frenzy. She called John, hoping he would answer because she needed help. When he did, she said, "Are you home?"

"Yes."

"I'll be there in a minute." She hung up.

As she raced down the stairs with Jasper beside her, she realized John must have wondered what was going on because she was usually fairly calm and rational, even when they'd met in the middle of her plumbing crisis. They got in her car, and she backed down the drive. When she turned left, a massive fallen tree across the road blocked her way. Now, she was pinned here.

She called John again. "I'm really sorry to bother you, but I'm at the inn. Well, I'm in my car in the inn's driveway because a tree's blocking the road. A window in the inn broke. I'm pretty sure you have plastic sheeting in your attic. Can I run over to get some from you?"

He said, "On my way," and ended the call.

Randi pulled forward into her usual spot. There was no point worrying about putting her car in a safe place because there wasn't one. She was surrounded by more giant trees.

As she got out, she heard those trees creaking as they swayed in the wind, an eerie sound that took the scene from Gothic to horror. She and Jasper ran back inside, her flashlight app lighting her path. Night had fallen while they'd been outside.

Randi stayed by the door as she waited for John. She knew it was silly, but this felt like a power outage since she was in a dark building, and that always freaked her out. She slept in the dark every night, but that was by choice and this wasn't.

A few minutes later, John opened the door, making the howling wind louder for a moment as he shook his umbrella outside before closing the door and muting the storm again. "It's nasty out here. Does it do this often in Tennessee?" He had brought a large flashlight, which, thankfully, flooded the room with light.

"More often than I'd like," she said. "But I guess almost every location has some kind of weather that someone may not like."

Jasper, too scared to greet his new friend, stayed by Randi's side.

"What did you bring?"

He held up a folded plastic tarp. "And some small tacks to hold it in place."

Randi started toward the stairs, her dog glued to her side. "It's upstairs. After we cover the window, I want to sweep up the glass that flew everywhere."

John kept pace with her.

"Jasper's going to hate this, but I'm going to need to shut him up in one of the other rooms upstairs because I don't want him to cut his paws."

She paused halfway down the hallway and opened the door.

Jasper looked at her and then at John like, *I don't know which way I want to go.*

She ushered John into the room. "Let's go far enough into the room that he follows us."

They stepped inside as lightning flashed, and Jasper started howling again.

"Okay, run and close the door. I don't want to leave him in there alone in a storm, but I have to protect him from the glass." Jasper moved slower than normal, so they managed to close the door before he could follow them out.

The dog's howling increased in volume. "We'll be right back, Jasper." He got quieter as though he understood.

Within a few minutes, they'd swept the glass to the side so they could both get in front of the window, and it wouldn't slice through their shoes. John held the tarp over the open window, and she tapped in the tacks around it to hold it securely. After that, Randi looked at the rain-soaked room and blew out a breath. "I hope the wood floors aren't destroyed."

John reached for the broom. "Let's clean up the rest of the glass and save Jasper. He isn't happy."

A beagle howl punctuated his comment.

"That's an understatement," she muttered. Randi grabbed paper towels and a trash bag from her cleaning cart, hoping he didn't notice it or comment on the broom. She couldn't think of any reasons she should have one at a property she represented.

John swept, and she held the dustpan to collect the glass. She carried it over to the trash bag on her cart and dumped it in there. Then they wiped down the wall and floor with her paper towels.

As they worked, he said, "From what I can tell by flashlight, this looks okay. It was just a few minutes from when you called to when we stopped the rain, so I think you're all right."

She was coming to that same conclusion herself.

He waved the light around over the floor as he stood. "These floors are beautiful. It's old-growth timber that you just don't see anymore."

She stood. "I think that's good for now. Let's grab Jasper and get out of here." She needed to get John back downstairs because while this hallway may appear old and unloved, many of the rooms, including the one her dog was in, had been cleaned.

Before she could worry any longer, Jasper kicked up his howling to a never-heard-before level.

"I need to keep him out of this room, just in case there's glass we can't see until there's sunlight shining through that window. We need to leave the inn to be safe."

"Good plan." John glanced around as they exited. "It looks nicer than I would expect. Have you been doing some sort of maintenance?"

She knew she should come one hundred percent clean. "I've

been working on some of the upstairs rooms. Dusting, sweeping—and other things."

"That's actually a good idea."

She stopped and looked up at him. "It is?" Had he figured out she wanted to buy it?

"It'll help someone in their decision to buy if they can see an inn that looks habitable instead of abandoned."

"Good point," she muttered as they continued down the hall. She should tell him about her dream to buy the inn, but every time she considered telling someone, it seemed like the more people who knew, the more chances she had of someone beating her to the purchase. And they might try to talk her out of her dream.

That was silly, of course, because Michelle had no desire to own the inn, and she'd supported Randi through motel improvements and getting her real estate license when others wondered why she'd do either. As an author, John likely faced doubters about his career.

She opened the door to what she knew Jasper thought of as a prison. He bounded out, jumped on her, then jumped on John. Jasper licked her arm as she reached down to pet him, acting as if he'd been in solitary confinement for a week.

Randi started toward the stairs. "My car isn't going anywhere tonight. Could you give me a ride to the motel? I know someone will clear out the tree when it's daylight, but I doubt anybody's going to get on it this time of night. You know, I should probably call the sheriff's office to let them know."

She picked up her phone and tapped the number for the sheriff's office, reporting the downed tree. "Let's get going. I'm wet enough already. I guess it won't matter if there's more."

"I have a giant umbrella I plan to share with you on the walk back to my house. It's one of those that you use when you're golfing."

"Are you a golfer?"

He laughed. "Not really, but I thought the umbrella was pretty awesome."

She laughed as they stepped out into the darkness, and the rain pelted them.

"Me either. My dad loves it."

"Same here. I can see the beauty in it. I mean, it's green, and you get to be outside. I enjoy both of those things, but the part of the game where you try to hit the little ball into the little cup doesn't work for me."

This was one of the first times Randi had seen a sense of humor in John, and she really liked it. She was about to speak when another gust came and blew the rain under the umbrella into her face.

She gasped and swiped at her cheeks. "Oh, nasty. I hope this ends soon."

Jasper ran ahead of them and then came back. She suspected he wanted them to hurry to get out of the storm.

John said, "I checked the forecast before I headed out the door. It looks like the bad weather won't last much longer."

Her dog splashed through a puddle, turned, and went through it again. "Oh no! Jasper's muddy. I'm sorry in advance for what's about to happen to your truck."

"I can put a blanket on the back seat."

"Is this the logical side that lets you plan out books and characters so that everything's in the right order?"

He laughed. "If only you knew. I'm a fairly messy writer. Maybe that's why I try to keep other things in my life in good shape."

Randi leaned over the seat to check on Jasper. "Again, I'm really sorry about the whole wet dog thing." They made their way down the soggy road, occasionally splashing through puddles, which reminded her again of the dog in the backseat.

"I grew up with three dogs, and we lived on a lake. If you only knew how many wet dogs I've had to take care of." He chuckled.

"So it's not a problem?"

"Not even a little one."

"I'm surprised you don't have a dog."

"This is going to come as a disappointment to you, but I'm probably more of a cat person."

She tried to picture him with a cat and couldn't quite get there. "In that case, why don't you have a cat?"

"I have been on the move for the last four or five years. I stay in one place for the winter and another in the summer. Sometimes, I only go somewhere for a month, like when I went to Bali. I spent about six weeks in northern Spain and Basque country. I've had a lot of fun."

John confirmed with every word that he was not someone who would stick around no matter what he said about buying the house. Randi fortified the walls around her heart. That was getting harder and harder because she knew he was someone she could easily fall for. He was easy on the eyes, but that wasn't the only reason. John was easy to be with, comfortable, and fun, and he had an air of excitement about him. Life would be an adventure if you were near him.

Maybe Michelle was right, and she'd already fallen for him.

They turned the corner, and the motel's lit-up sign led them the rest of the way.

"I live in the owner's quarters that are connected to the back of the office, so pull around behind the office. And I know you don't care about the dirty dog being in here, but can I at least wash the blanket that's on your back seat?"

"I don't have a washer and dryer, so I will happily turn the blanket over to you. I haven't decided what to do about that since my plans haven't been finalized. And there doesn't seem to be a laundromat in town, either."

The time limit on his stay always made her put up her guard. *Breathe, Randi.* He'd said he'd like to buy the house. They hadn't finalized the deal yet, but she hoped he would. "You're right about having to work to find a laundromat. It's probably a thirty-minute drive in a couple of directions. Just bring your stuff over and wash them here. I have a commercial-sized washer and dryer for the motel. Most of that laundry gets done in the early afternoon, so morning or later in the evening works."

"Thanks. I may take you up on that as a temporary fix. You know, a laundromat sounds like a good business for someone to put in the town."

"Oh, we used to have one. The owner retired, and you know how it is with a town that doesn't have much going on. Either somebody didn't have the money to take it over, or the people with money didn't have any interest."

John asked, "Do you want to grab the dog or the blanket?"

She was about to say that Jasper would just run to the front door, but a flash of lightning, followed closely by a loud boom, made the dog cower and whimper. He might run off if she let him out off-leash, even if he wouldn't usually consider it.

She handed John the key. "If you unlock the door, I'll carry him inside." She ran through the pouring rain with her dog, and already inside, John opened the door for them, closing it quickly after they'd entered.

"Whew!" She set Jasper down, and the dog stood there looking at her as if to say, *Make this storm stop!*

"Point me to the towels, and I'll grab one for you to dry him off."

"Thank you! They're stacked on a shelf in the linen closet around the corner." Randi pointed beyond her tiny living area, which seemed even smaller with John in it, to the hallway that led to her equally small bedroom and bath. Her style was simple with casual neutrals with pops of her favorite color—yellow. "I'd usually give him a bath, but he doesn't like baths, and the thunder has really scared him."

When John returned, she rubbed the towel on her dog, wondering if she should offer John a snack or something to drink. He stood still as though he didn't know what to do next either.

"Jasper's almost dry." She felt silly after she spoke because, in her nervousness, she'd stated the obvious.

John had asked her to dinner at his house, but she'd turned him down. She knew that had been a monumental mistake because she did want to spend time with him. Before she could stop herself, Randi blurted out, "I have hot chocolate and could make a bowl of popcorn. There's a mystery movie I've been wanting to watch. That is if you'd like to stay for a little while." She turned to see what his response would be.

His eyes lit up. "I can make the snack while you stay near Jasper. Would that work for you?"

She relaxed. He *did* want to spend more time with her. "Thank you!" Randi sat on the couch, and Jasper leaned against her legs. "You're okay, boy." She scratched him behind his ears.

John found milk in the fridge and poured it into a pan on the stove.

"Homemade hot chocolate?"

"Definitely. It's much better."

"You're probably going to frown on the microwave popcorn I was planning to use."

He laughed. "That's fine."

"In that case, it's in a box in the cupboard to your right."

"And I should have asked before now, but do you have cocoa and sugar?"

"You'll find everything you need for the hot chocolate there too."

Jasper seemed to be calming down now that they were home. Thunder followed by a gust of wind had him push against her more tightly, but he hadn't started howling again. The driving rain hadn't slowed down, but that didn't seem to bother him as much.

Randi leaned back on the couch. This had been a long day, but it was ending better. She glanced over at John. Maybe there would be another kiss before he left.

He turned toward her. "Everything okay?"

Randi felt her face heating. Could he read her mind? "Great. Thank you for helping."

Just as John put the popcorn in the microwave, the lights dimmed and then returned to full power. "Whew! I thought the power was going to go out. That almost ruined our evening."

"We'd have a lukewarm drink and about a tablespoon of popped corn." He chuckled.

The power flickered, and the room went black. Randi sat still, hoping it would come back on. A bolt of lightning gave the only light to the room.

She stood. "Rats! I have emergency kits that I deliver to every cottage when this happens. The power doesn't go out very often, but when it does, guests appreciate everything in the kit."

John's phone flashlight came on. "Our movie night seems to be gone, but I could deliver the kits instead so Jasper doesn't get wet again or left alone."

Her dog was still glued to her side, but when John knelt to pet him, Jasper leaned into him. "Actually, Jasper loves you too. The guests know me, so I should probably be the one who delivers the kits. Would you stay with my dog while I do that?"

John sat on the couch where Randi had been. "Jasper, are you willing to have me as your dog sitter for a few minutes?"

"I'll be right back. I have five occupied cottages, so this won't take long. I'm glad this isn't the night before a big wedding." Using the flashlight she kept in a kitchen drawer, one that was much more powerful than the one on her phone, Randi went down the hall, grabbed three of the plastic bins, brought them to the living room, then went back for the other two.

"Whoa. What's in there?"

"Two battery-powered lanterns, a USB charger for devices—I keep those charged up and ready, snack bars, individual bags of chips and pretzels, and water bottles. Sitting in the dark in a strange place can be scary and disorienting. I want guests to leave with good feelings about the motel."

"That's genius."

Randi felt a flush of pride at his compliment. She did the best she could with the motel and hoped to bring this level of service and more to the inn.

Ten minutes later, she had run back and forth from here to the cottages, handing one to a guest then picking up another. Everyone was thrilled when she explained what the box contained.

When she'd finished and returned to her home, John stood. "I think it's time for me to leave. I should make sure my house is secure. I checked the weather report on my phone, and this mess is supposed to be ending soon." He reached down to pat the dog. "You're going to be okay now, boy." To Randi, he said, "Could I borrow one of those kits?"

She laughed. "Your phone's going to run out of juice pretty soon, and you'd be in the dark."

"I hadn't thought to buy flashlights or other emergency supplies, so I appreciate this." He hesitated for a moment before continuing. "Maybe we could move the movie night to another day."

"I'd like that." She hoped what they had would be given time to grow.

When John started toward the door, Randi remembered their conversation on the way here. "The blanket in your car."

"You're right! I'll be right back with it."

John stepped out into the night and quickly returned. "The rain has stopped." She took the blanket from him and set it on a table beside the door. "I'll wash this tomorrow." She waited to see if he would kiss her. Seconds turned into a minute with neither of them moving.

Just when John took a step toward her, a loud thunderclap sounded, and Jasper howled. John turned away and started back to his truck. "I'll probably see you tomorrow."

He would if she had anything to say about it.

CHAPTER FOURTEEN

*J*ohn drove around the curve that followed the lake. Two men were using chainsaws to cut through the fallen tree's branches. He parked at the side of the road, then got out and walked over to them.

"Do you guys need any help?" he asked when they spotted him and turned off the noisy equipment.

One of the men said, "We don't have an extra saw. But we could use help moving the pieces off the road when we've made more headway. Can you come back in a half hour or so?"

"I'm just going up here for a bit." He motioned toward the inn. "I'll be back to help."

"Sounds good. Thanks."

John walked up the driveway, noticing even more on foot that an overwhelming amount of foliage had overtaken what he knew had once been a beautiful approach to an amazing old building.

This time, instead of going to the front door, he pushed his way through to the side of the building where he could see the tarp-covered corner Randi had mentioned. A stone bench peered out from under the weeds, but an area the width of one person had been cleared. Randi must sit here sometimes.

He continued around back to check on the window where they'd done the temporary patch last night. A few other windows had small cracks in them but hadn't broken through.

Anyone who took on the job of reviving this inn would be taking on a lot. He already had a job. Some people didn't think being a writer was work, but in addition to making up stories out of thin air, he had to handle all the marketing and other tasks associated with running his writing business.

Sure, he was grateful he could have more free time than someone who worked from eight to five for someone else, but sometimes his hours far exceeded that. Occasionally, late evening and weekend work were required to meet deadlines. And his writing didn't happen just when the muse struck because full-time authors had to work even when the muse was on vacation. But living alone, he saw no reason not to work if he didn't have anything else to do.

And his profession did give him moments like this when he could sit and just be with no boss watching him.

He went back to the bench he'd passed and pulled away the vines that had done their best to overtake it. They fought him, but after a battle of pulling and tugging for a good ten to fifteen minutes, he had a pile of weeds and could see the whole bench for what he guessed was the first time in decades.

Watching the building his ancestors had built—the one that he'd grown up with stories about—collapse into the ground from neglect, or worse, to be torn down, was something he couldn't get past.

Even though he hadn't signed the contract yet, he knew he was going to buy the house he was living in. The moment he'd stepped inside, he'd felt like he was home. That hadn't happened before, not in all his travels. And, as much as the thought overwhelmed him, the only way he could find to save the inn was to buy it too. His books had been popular, so he had enough income to do that.

He couldn't save every old building an ancestor had lived in throughout the country, but the inn had been special to him when he was growing up. He could still see his grandfather's excited face as he shared stories about this place that he'd also heard about as a child. But owning an inn hadn't been on his bucket list.

Did he want to be an innkeeper? The answer kept coming back as *no*.

"Is everything okay?"

Randi's voice startled him as she appeared through the jungle.

"The men at the road said you were here, and you don't have a key to the building, so ..." She laughed. "I followed the broken vines."

"It's hard to imagine this being a cleared walkway. I just wanted to take a look at the damage in the daylight, and I found this bench. I can picture my great-great-grandmother sitting here after walking over from her house. I'd like to clear the path between my house and the inn. And I do want to buy the house. We can close on that as soon as the documents are ready."

"That's great!" Randi's face lit up. "I'm glad you're staying." She sat next to him. "It's a beautiful old building, and the land is extra special." She sighed. "For some reason, I'm getting more calls about the inn lately and the property the inn sits on."

John pushed thoughts of Randi away to focus on the inn. Maybe he wouldn't have to buy it. If there were more calls about the inn, maybe a boutique hotel group would buy it and turn it into a spectacular destination hotel.

Randi's voice sounded strained. "One person seems serious. It may not be for sale for much longer. He would tear it down."

That hardened his resolve to buy it.

He hadn't told Randi about his family's connection to this

building before because he'd been interrupted, and it hadn't seemed important. Now, it felt as if he'd missed his chance to gracefully tell Randi and the town. He knew Greg wasn't one to spread gossip, so he was probably the only one who knew.

John shifted in his seat. His confession may seem like he'd been in town and even with her under false pretenses. "My great-great-grandparents built the inn. They were the first owners."

Randi stared at him. "You didn't think it was important to mention that?"

He tried for an answer that didn't make him sound like he'd been keeping secrets, especially after that kiss had changed their relationship. In what way, he still wasn't sure. "I thought I was just passing through. Then I started to tell you once but was interrupted." He shrugged. "I honestly didn't think anyone would care. It was a long time ago. The inn was gambled away, and they left town."

She took a few deep breaths. Then she turned back toward the inn, not saying anything for a couple of minutes. Her proper businesslike tone had replaced her earlier friendliness. "You're right. I … just feel a connection to this old girl."

He'd thought he was in deep trouble. Maybe he was. "I truly didn't plan to hide anything. I told Greg when I met him on my first day here."

Randi put her hand on his arm. "I'm sure his mother wishes he wasn't so good at keeping secrets."

He liked her nearness. It also made him wonder if he'd misread her response to the kiss. She'd been friendly last night, but he hadn't been sure about what his next move should be. Maybe she did care for him beyond friendship and business.

"It's good to know that the town's sheriff knows how to keep things private." John pointed to the corner of the building. "That must be where the tree fell months ago. It looks like you did a good job of securing the corner."

"Greg helped me with that one. I didn't notice the damage for probably three or four days, but fortunately, the tree branch must have fallen after the rain, so there wasn't any water damage inside. Just the animals that used it as a ladder to the inside of the inn." She smiled.

Randi removed her hand, and he immediately missed her warmth. "I'll have the glass later today to fix the window, but I'm probably better off letting the wood dry out for another day or two before I attempt to do anything with it."

"That makes sense." Their conversation felt insignificant in the middle of the monumental changes and decisions he had in his life. The house. The inn. *And Randi.*

He didn't know if he should talk about their kiss to break the ice or keep going with their businesslike conversation. He chickened out and decided to bring up the thought about the inn that kept coming back to him. "I know there's been interest in the land, but that's a big maybe this far from the city. Don't you agree? It sounds like a good idea to someone in Nashville, but would they follow through and even come out to see the property?"

Her shoulders relaxed. She'd become more attached to the building than he'd realized.

"Randi, do you think someone will come along who wants to save this place?"

She answered with surprising conviction in her voice. "Absolutely. She's a structurally sound old building. Yes, she's showing her age and neglect, but I believe someone will buy her and bring her back to life."

"That sounds positive. Is it because you're a real estate agent, and you think every property you represent will sell? Or do you really believe that?"

She seemed to hesitate for a minute. "No, I really do believe the inn will sell to an owner who preserves it and soon." Her excitement vanished, replaced by sadness. "If there's enough time before a teardown buyer makes a solid offer."

John could see flecks of the lake between some of the tree branches and brush. Between the view and the building, he knew this had been a special place. "This must have been a place worth the trip."

"I agree. I would have loved to have been at the Two Hearts Inn when there were ladies and gentlemen in their finery. I've seen photos of a rose garden behind this bench, but there's no sign of it now."

He didn't remember anything there but more vines, weeds, and brush. John turned, and that's exactly what he saw. As he swiveled back, he got an idea that felt a little like something he might have done in high school, but he scooted closer to her at the same time, hoping it would seem like a natural motion. He wanted Randi to make the next move, but he would do this much to see what her response would be.

"I like your idea for the paddle boats on the lake."

Randi looked at him with shock. "We never talked about paddle boats."

So much for waiting for her response to his moving closer. She wouldn't even notice because he'd said something he shouldn't have. He'd read that when he'd been standing at her check-in desk, but he probably shouldn't have. "I saw your list when I was at the motel. I think it's great that you're putting together marketing ideas for potential buyers." He didn't add that some of her ideas had helped inspire him about what was possible.

Randi nodded. "Right. *Marketing ideas.* Thank you."

John realized the chainsaw had stopped along with warmth in this conversation. "I need to go over to help the guys. I told them I'd move some of the branches when they were done."

She bit her lip as she watched him stand. It felt like they were at a turning point, and he didn't know his next steps. He hoped he'd figure out the answer to at least one of his big life questions. The one about Randi was at the top of his list. Was she interested in him, or just humoring a client?

Randi watched John disappear into the wall of green without a word. He kept adding checkmarks in the nice column. Helping clear the tree would make him more involved in the town, so that was a good thing.

He'd come to her rescue last night. Then it had felt almost like a date when he was making the hot chocolate and popcorn. But today, she wasn't sure.

After a quick check inside to make sure everything seemed stable, she'd go to *Dinah's Place* for lunch. Michelle would be waiting for an update.

Randi needed advice.

CHAPTER FIFTEEN

Randi picked up her phone as she drove from the inn to Dinah's Place.

"Can you give me a full tour of the inn?" a voice she thought belonged to John asked.

She pulled the phone away from her ear and quickly checked the screen to see the name. It was definitely him, but his question didn't make any sense.

"You've been in the inn a couple of times. I gave you a quick tour downstairs, and you were upstairs last night."

Silence greeted her. Then, his next words shook her to her core. "I may want to buy it."

Randi pulled to the side of the road and stopped. "*Buy* the inn? The house *and* the inn?" Shock ran through her. She knew it was irrational, but she felt like someone she'd trusted wanted to take the inn away from her. This wasn't a stranger on her phone who'd found an ad online. This was the man she'd foolishly fallen for.

"Can I see it?"

As the real estate agent, she couldn't say anything but, "Of course. I can meet you there in a half hour." As the woman who'd put her life on hold to save enough to buy the inn, she wanted to shout, "No! It's going to be mine soon."

~

John walked the perimeter of the inn's dining room. He'd seen it before, but only as a visitor, not as a possible owner. The massive room could easily hold a couple hundred people seated, possibly many more. He'd never had to estimate a restaurant's capacity before.

He'd never had to do any of this before, and everywhere he looked, he saw work and more work. But more than that, he saw the situation at the end of all the renovation and repairs—the job of running the place.

He wanted to be an author. He didn't want to be an innkeeper. This must be the dumbest thing he had ever gotten himself in the middle of, but here he was.

He needed to save this piece of both the town's and his family's history. It seemed like no one else was going to do it, so he had to do it.

Randi pointed up to the ceiling. "I think the chandeliers will be okay once the power's on again. I got up on a ladder once and checked them out." She shrugged. "But I'm not an electrician. You know that the entire inn will have to be rewired, right?"

He nodded. Electric. Plumbing. New roof. Air conditioning and heating. The price of a heating and cooling system alone for a building this size would be massive. He'd done well with his books, but this could take every dollar he'd saved. Maybe even more.

He was pulled back to the inn itself by Randi. She practically gushed when she talked about the inn's features. That must be what made her an excellent real estate agent. When she went on again about another detail, this time the lakeview windows—he could picture her vision for the inn. Was there a view of the lake today? No, but she painted it so clearly that he could almost see the sun glinting off the water.

Then he realized she hadn't been this way about the rental properties she'd shown him. She'd been more matter-of-fact, telling him about the property's qualities, even pointing out when one of the small houses didn't have a dishwasher.

Here, she was enthusiasm all the way. It made him feel like he needed to get a little more of that for himself. Finally, when she pointed out two more things as they were leaving the room, he stopped and faced her. "You love this place, don't you?"

She looked up at him and slowly nodded her head. "Yeah, I do. I wanted … never mind, it doesn't matter now. Let's continue upstairs."

Her footsteps slowed with each step up the grand staircase, and she was fidgeting with her hands like she didn't know whether to put them at her side or twist them in front of herself.

Maybe the upstairs was worse than he realized. He'd been down the one hallway by flashlight. He actually had very little idea of what the upstairs looked like when he thought about it. One room had a broken window. Another one had a hole from a tree.

A wide, long hallway with crown molding at the ceiling and wide base moldings that met what was left of the carpet, he remembered that much. This place was highly decorated everywhere you turned. He hoped he'd be able to salvage some, if not all, of that.

When they stepped on the second floor, Randi nervously licked her lips and paused. Then she abruptly turned to the right—the opposite direction of where he'd gone the night of the storm.

"I've done some work on the rooms near the one you were in the other night. Before we go there, I'm going to show you one that's untouched other than a quick clearing out of spiders and other creepy crawlies that had taken up residence."

"Let's see what I have to do here." When she opened the door to the room, John gasped. "This is worse than I imagined. Even by flashlight, the other room looked much better than this." Other than the bed against the wall, the remaining furniture was grouped in the center of the room. Litter from who knows what was sprinkled over the wood floor. The bed looked like it had been home to more than a few critters. And the fireplace had half-burned logs in it with the ash they'd left behind.

"Now, there's something I need to tell you." She twisted her hands in front of herself. Randi's nervousness returned. "Follow me." She led him out to the hall again and toward the other end of the hallway. "I know this next guestroom will surprise you after the one I just showed you. I've done some cleanup upstairs. Quite a few of the rooms are ... better."

"You cleaned? I thought there was something terrible you were going to point out."

She giggled, but it oozed nervousness and tension. "It's more than you realize. I've actually painted some of the rooms and worked on the plumbing in the bathrooms. I can't test the plumbing with the water off, but I know what I'm doing, so it's correct."

Okay, this was very strange because it meant she had not only invested time but also her own money in the property. "Did the owner ask you to do that?"

She shook her head. "He doesn't know about it. He's never set foot in Two Hearts or even in Tennessee. He lives in Oregon and inherited the inn from his family."

John stopped, but she continued down the hall. "Randi, stop, please. What aren't you telling me? What's going on?"

She opened the door to one of the rooms, swinging it wide, and gestured for him to enter. "Please," she said, then gave a frustrated sigh.

He did as she asked. When he stepped into the room, his jaw dropped. She hadn't just painted. It looked like a guest could stay here. Now. This second.

He turned to face her. "I don't understand. If the owner didn't pay you to do this—"

"I wanted to buy the inn!" she shouted at him. Then she dropped her voice. "I'm sorry. I'm sorry." Randi stepped back. "I never should have told you that. Pretend I didn't say anything. I just broke about a million codes of the ethical conduct of a real estate agent. Laws, I'm sure. Please, please don't tell anybody."

His gaze went first from her to the room and back.

"Why *haven't* you bought it?"

She blew out a deep breath. "In about six to eight months, if I have a few higher valued real estate properties close—like the lake houses in Two Hearts or other large houses in the nearby towns—then my bank account would have enough in it for me to outright buy the inn. I don't think financing is going to be possible, not with a regular loan at least, because it's not habitable."

He gestured to the room around them. "I know what you mean, but this looks amazing."

"In short, it's an inn that's not anywhere near being able to bring in income. I don't think it would look like a good investment for a bank or any other lender."

When he saw this room, he wanted to argue her point, but then he remembered everywhere else he'd been on the property. "I see what you mean. I'm going to be honest with you now. I really don't want to buy the inn."

Her brow furrowed. "I don't understand. You just told me you *want* to buy it. That's why we're here."

"I don't want to *buy* this. What I want is for it not to fall into the ground or be plowed under by someone who thinks the land alone is great. I want to save the building my great-great-grandparents built."

"So you aren't going to buy it?" Randi stared at him in disbelief. "I have two possible buyers who have called more than once. One of them asked for the plat map of the land but not for photos of the inside of the building. The other one actually said he would tear down the building. In short, I think a good offer is about to come in for this place, an offer the owner will accept. The land itself is special, but both of them would tear down the inn."

She raised her arms in frustration. "I don't want to lose this beautiful old building. Opening it again would mean more for the town than one wealthy family's estate would. Having more guests here would bring in money for lots of other businesses."

He nodded. "My concern isn't so much restoring the building. It's running it as an inn."

She had a sad smile. "Running it is the least of my concerns because I'm already running the motel. This property is larger, but it's the same basic principles."

He sighed. "I keep coming back to the fact that I'm an author. I love what I do. I'm happy to do something on the side, but I don't want a new profession. Being an innkeeper would be a full-time job."

"Then you aren't buying it?" She sounded both sad and a little happy. Her phone chimed with an incoming message and then again a few seconds later. She checked it with a frown and then slid the phone back into her pocket.

"I don't know. I told my grandfather I was." John wandered out of the room and into the hallway.

"Does that matter?" Randi followed her client out the guest room door.

"Once you tell him something, it's written in stone. He's going to ask me about it every time I talk to him."

"That isn't enough reason to change the direction of your life."

"No, but the stories I heard when I was a kid are. The

excitement he had about this old place ..." John shook his head. "I think I have to save the inn."

She said, "Good, because the messages I just got were from one of those people who want the land. He's coming out this weekend from Nashville to walk the land with his architect. I suspect he'll make an offer soon. The clock is ticking on saving this place."

They went downstairs in silence. When they reached the bottom, they both stopped, and Randi stared up at him. Should he kiss her again? No. He needed for her to initiate anything more. He wasn't the kind of man who chased after a woman who wasn't interested. He cleared his throat. The inn, Morgan. Focus on the inn. John said, "I'm going to have to think about this purchase overnight. It's a big decision."

Randi looked as if she was about to burst into tears.

Nice going, Morgan.

CHAPTER SIXTEEN

andi held it together, even managing to fake a smile as John opened the door to leave.

John turned toward her as if he wanted to say something but then shook his head and left. The solid sound of the large wooden door closing was magnified in the empty room.

She turned around to imagine the inn one last time as hers. She could still picture it as she had the first time she'd walked in. Instead of being overwhelmed by the cobwebs, she'd seen beyond the grime to a flourishing inn with people, fresh flowers on a table, and laughter. The inn had felt happy to her.

At that moment, she'd taken on the dream of bringing the Two Hearts Inn back to its former glory.

When Randi heard the crunch of tires on gravel as John drove away, she tried to focus on the beauty around her for a distraction. This place she'd come to love couldn't stop her heart from breaking.

A guttural sob brought her to her knees. She'd lost John *and* the inn. Randi sat on the floor, bent over with her face in her hands. Tears poured down her cheeks. Jasper whimpered beside her, clearly wanting to help.

Randi gulped for air as her world crashed down around her. Everything she'd worked for this year. All the hours she'd put into real estate and this building. That was all for nothing.

She tried for a cheerful tone. "I'm going to look on the bright side." There must be one. "Jasper, I'll have more time for taking you on walks."

He snuggled closer. Even her dog wasn't buying that as an upside when she felt so sad.

"Maybe I'll learn to cook better." The memory of John standing at his stove stirring the sauce flashed into her mind.

"Bad idea. Let's plan a trip to the beach during the slow month of January. You'd enjoy running on the sand." The closest beach to her would be in Florida, which brought back John's words about living there.

"This isn't helping." *Focus on work, Randi.* She could paint the motel. Something about the repetitive motion of painting calmed her down.

Jasper rested his head on her leg. "Good, boy. You're always there for me, aren't you?"

She ran her hand over his smooth fur. "We're going to get through this together."

She tried to slow her breathing, to calm herself. "Let's look on the bright side." She inhaled then exhaled. After doing that several times, she began to feel lightheaded. That hadn't helped.

Randi stretched out on the floor. Her dog was her only companion, her romance with John had been nothing more than a fantasy, and she was back to where she'd been in business a year ago.

A new wave of tears threatened.

She'd fallen for a man who only saw her as his real estate agent, someone who could write up the offer on the inn. And the house? She just realized that he might not want both it and the inn. He could renovate the inn then hire a team to run the place or even sell it. A ready-to-go property would be much more saleable. A boutique hotel chain might be interested.

Would he even stay in town now?

Did that even matter? She had thought he was interested in her, but maybe he'd just been carried away by emotion.

She'd read every smile as connection, every shared moment as possibility, but she'd just been the woman with the keys.

"Jasper, what are we going to do? You love him just as much as I do." Her dog sighed.

Randi sniffed and reached into the tote bag beside her to find the packet of tissues. As she wiped her tears away and blew her nose, she wondered what to do next. Her long-term plans had all focused on this property. Every waking moment that wasn't for one of her other businesses centered on the inn.

"It's time to move on." She patted Jasper's head before she stood and pulled out her phone. She tried to picture her future changed, but she couldn't. Maybe Michelle would have advice.

Her phone rang as she pulled it out of the bag to call her friend. John's name showed on the screen. Should she answer? The phone rang a second and third time. It felt like nothing good could come of talking to him right now. Her finger hovered over the button to end the call.

With a sigh, she answered. John may have broken her heart, but he was still a client. "What can I help you with?" The perky tone sounded over the top. She wandered over to a window and rubbed the dirt in a circle to clear it enough to peer through.

"Randi?"

She nodded, then realized he couldn't see her. Randi dropped her voice to what she hoped sounded more normal. "Yes, John. What do you need?" She tried for a straightforward, businesslike tone, but her voice wavered at the end.

She hoped his request would be easy because she didn't have much to give right now.

"I'm sorry." His tone was more personal than she'd expected.

Not at all the proper voice she expected now that they were only involved in simple real estate transactions.

"About?" Was he apologizing for taking her inn or breaking her heart? Then she realized he didn't know she'd fallen for him. Hiding her heart had been a good idea.

"If I'd realized …" John paused, and she heard chirping birds.

"Where are you?"

"The Lake Park. I came here after I left the inn. I had to gather my thoughts."

She knew the feeling.

His next words surprised her. "Will you meet me at the stone bench beside the inn tomorrow morning?" His warmth lured her in, but her first response was to shout *No!*

Her mouth said, "I can do that. Ten o'clock?"

"That's fine. And, Randi, I'm looking forward to seeing you then." He ended the call.

A thread of hope wove through her. Maybe there was still a chance that things could work out. She had no idea how, but she grabbed that whisper of hope and held onto it with both hands.

CHAPTER SEVENTEEN

John tucked his phone in his pocket. He felt more confused than he'd ever been in his life. Randi had sounded happier by the end of their call as if she'd been glad to talk to him even after he'd hurt her feelings.

Being here in nature at the lake park had given him time to realize that he wanted to pursue Randi. Woo her. He could send her a bouquet of flowers at the motel. Then he would ask her to dinner. She'd turned down his offer of another meal at his house, but maybe she'd agree to pizza or something fancier in the city. He wouldn't be pushy, but he couldn't just walk away without trying.

Maybe she needed time to fall for him.

At some point, Randi had become more important than the inn. But the inn seemed to stand between them.

He had to process all of it.

It turned out they both wanted to save the inn, but she was the one who actually wanted to take care of the day-to-day operations and run it from that point on, whereas he would rather walk away once the renovation was complete.

The only thing good about him buying the inn is that it

would be saved. He'd have to explore new horizons as an innkeeper and put his author career on hold. Neither was something he was looking forward to.

Judging from the plumbing incident when he first met Randi, older properties required frequent repairs and constant upkeep. He pictured her soaked with water. She'd been a fighter as she worked through that problem, and she'd succeeded.

That was one of the many things he loved about her.

Repairs like that at the inn, though, would cause his work to suffer. That meant his income could suffer, which also meant he would be relying on an inn in a small town for his complete livelihood. An inn he had no idea how to run.

The situation was spiraling out of control, and he didn't know how to reel it back in.

On top of all of that, he'd thought she felt something for him, but maybe it was just their mutual connection to the inn. He'd surprised her when he kissed her, but she had responded to his kiss.

He needed answers before morning. There *had* to be answers to his dilemma. When he wrote a book, he could make all the pieces fit together by the end. He knew life wasn't like a fictional story, but there had to be a way to make this situation better. To not leave everything with Randi in such chaos.

It seemed to come back to the inn every time. He needed input, to talk this over with someone.

He had a good relationship with his parents, but calling one of them to ask about buying the inn wouldn't work. It had been clear growing up that his grandfather had found someone who also loved history in his grandson but not in his son. His grandfather would tell him to buy it without asking about the condition or how much it cost.

His father had heard the same stories, but they hadn't caught his imagination as they had John's. His dad would tell him to walk away from the inn.

And his best friend had new baby twins, so he was completely caught up in his own life situation right now.

In Two Hearts, Greg was his closest connection, and someone he thought might eventually become a good friend. John took out his phone to send the sheriff a text and started walking home. Then he got in his truck to drive to Dinah's. He needed to eat whether or not the sheriff was going to be joining him there, and he wasn't in the mood to cook himself.

A reply came as he pulled into the parking lot. *I can be there in 10.*

John knew from experience that the restaurant could get busy at lunchtime, so he went in to get them a table. He claimed one next to the wall when someone left, glad to have a little more privacy than a center-of-the-room table would.

Greg came through the door right on schedule. When he sat, he said, "I'd better get my food ordered because I never know what's happening next. I do have other employees now, but all it takes is a hay bale on the highway or some other situation to pull me away from my food."

John laughed. "I'm glad you could meet me for lunch."

They both chose the special, which turned out to be meatloaf, mac and cheese, and green beans. Then the sheriff gave John a long look.

"Is this just a casual 'wanted to see you again before you left town,' or is something wrong? I know you moved into the house on the lake."

It figures that he'd know everything that went on in this town. Or almost everything. "I'm not leaving."

"You're staying?" Greg grinned. "You were sure you were just visiting. Of course, the house rental surprised me."

"I feel a connection to this place because of my family roots. And now I've made a decision to do something else that I'm regretting before it's even done."

"That doesn't sound good."

Their food arrived, and they both ate a few bites before the conversation continued.

John set down his fork. "I'm hoping you won't mind being my sounding board."

Greg glanced over at him as he scooped up a bite of mac and cheese. "Not at all."

"I told you how my family owned the inn."

"Yes."

"I mistakenly didn't tell Randi."

Greg did a slow nod. "And that matters because she's become a friend?"

"More than a friend."

Greg raised an eyebrow. "Interesting. Continue."

"Worse than that, I don't want to be an innkeeper."

Greg raised an eyebrow. "You're buying the inn, but you don't want to buy the inn?"

John blew out a breath. "That sounds ridiculous, doesn't it."

Greg shrugged. "I've heard worse, but then I'm in a different line of work."

John smiled at his new friend's words. Greg probably saw all kinds of odd things as sheriff. "I just don't want the inn to crumble to the ground or to be demolished."

"So that's the dilemma. You're buying something you don't want."

"A hundred percent."

He didn't know if he should reveal Randi's interest in the property, but Greg needed that for context. John leaned forward and lowered his voice. "Once I'd said I wanted to buy the inn—and Randi did nothing wrong because she didn't try to dissuade me from making that offer—she told me she'd wanted to buy it."

Greg considered his words, then nodded. "That kind of makes sense since she already runs a lodging property. A natural extension."

"Exactly."

"So then, why hasn't she?"

"She's been saving but doesn't have enough money yet."

Greg leaned back in his chair. "Now I understand why she's seemed so busy. I feel like I've seen her everywhere. In the past, she'd just be at the motel and show a few properties in town. But I heard she'd sold some things in neighboring towns too. Every weekend, she's out working in real estate." He gave a rueful smile. "She was saving for it, and you came in and swooped it up."

"Exactly. What should I do?"

"Well, that's easy. Just change your mind. It becomes hers when she has enough money. I doubt there's anyone else that wants to save that old place." Greg started eating again as he listened.

"That's actually the problem and the reason I called you. There's someone who may be interested in the land because it's a pretty piece of property on the lake, but they'll tear it down and build a lakefront mansion."

Greg winced. "That isn't what we want, is it? To tear things down. If it were in worse shape, I think I could support that, but I believe it's salvageable."

"I do too."

"So let me get this straight. Randi doesn't have enough money to buy it, but you do. She wants it, but you don't." He poured ketchup on his meatloaf and took a bite of it.

"That's all correct."

"But someone else may want to tear it down, which means nobody gets to keep the inn."

"Correct. But it's not a done deal."

"No, it's not. But once they make an offer, then it would be gone for everyone. I know for a fact that the inn's current owner isn't interested in the history. He told me he just wanted the money. He inherited the inn from his grandfather, who inherited it from his parents. He wants it sold and doesn't care who it sells to."

"You've talked to him?"

"He's called a couple of times to make sure the building was secure. I drive by every once in a while to make sure it's locked and there aren't any squatters." Greg tapped his fingers on the tabletop as he considered the situation. "I think you told me you were handy with fixing things. At least that isn't a problem."

"I can tinker around on the place and do a lot of the work myself. I'm not an electrician or a plumber, so they may need to be brought in at some point, but I could do a lot of other work around my writing. At least when it comes to the renovation."

"I really hate to see that place demolished. I have an idea, but you may not like it." Greg's phone rang, and he answered. "Okay, okay, I'm on my way." As he stood, he said, "I'm sorry I can't stay to hash this out."

"Are you kidding, Greg? You said you have the answer, and now you can't tell me?"

Greg leaned closer. "Split it."

"What?"

Greg looked down at his phone, where messages must be coming in. He looked up. "I've got to run. But you buy half. Let her buy half. Split it. Everybody's happy."

John stared after the sheriff as he went out the door, not blinking and definitely not moving.

That had not occurred to him or, he was sure, to Randi. He could help put the inn back together, and then Randi could run it. He'd get some part of the profits.

This could be perfect—*if* she was interested.

He hoped she was, because the idea of doing all this on his own wasn't something he was looking forward to.

With any luck he was about to make tomorrow brighter.

CHAPTER EIGHTEEN

John sat on the stone bench, waiting nervously for Randi to arrive and wondering how he would propose the split ownership. He felt like he'd come to some big decisions during the night and hoped he understood her as well as he thought he did. If she thought that was a good idea, he had a plan ready for what he'd propose next.

As a writer, you would think he'd have a great plan for starting the conversation. Words that would help her see this arrangement could work.

Nothing had come to him overnight. At least nothing more about the inn had. At about midnight, he'd realized he had a different offer in mind. He'd texted Randi to move their appointment to noon. Then he'd hopped into his truck and been in Nashville when stores opened this morning.

He checked the time on his phone. Five minutes to twelve. He'd barely made it here in time for their meeting.

Jasper crashed through the brush. Then the dog jumped onto the bench, sat beside John, and licked his cheek.

"Jasper!" John laughed. "Where's your mom?"

Randi trod through the brush a moment later. Her eyes were

red and swollen, probably from tears she'd shed over losing her dream. The one he'd stolen from her.

He touched the seat to the other side of him. "Please join me."

She hesitated, and he hated that he'd done this to her.

"Please?"

"I will sit, but I'd like to say that I've been selfish for wanting to buy this. Your offer to buy the inn is gracious and will save the inn."

He couldn't help but ask. "Is that the only reason you wanted it?"

"Honestly, the motel is small, and I can't expand. I want to grow to the point where I can have employees to help with day-to-day tasks, but I'm limited by the number of guests I can have at one time. That puts a ceiling on my income. Having the inn would have changed everything." She sat beside him, keeping to herself with her hands in her lap. "But that's not to be, and I need to move on." She muttered something else.

"What?"

"I need to move on about many things." She stared at her hands.

"I have an idea. Actually, Greg gave it to me. You would enjoy running the inn, right?"

She nodded, still not looking up.

"I don't want to run the inn. Especially not alone. I need a partner."

She looked at him. "I don't understand."

"Can we each buy half of the inn? Be business partners? I help when needed, but I can still be a writer. You'll run the inn."

A smile began at the corners of her mouth, then her whole face lit up. "That's genius. We both get what we want."

"Truthfully, I only wanted to save it. You'll have more of the day-to-day responsibilities. I may enjoy helping in the kitchen sometimes, though."

Randi laughed, and he was so glad to see her sadness sliding away. "The kitchen isn't my best place." She put out her hand. "Partners."

He slid his hand in hers and held on. "I'd like to propose more than a business partnership," he said softly. He let go of Randi's hand and knelt in front of her, tugging the small pink velvet box out of his pocket as he did.

She gasped, and fresh tears came to her eyes. He hoped they were tears of joy.

"I know this is sudden. But I'd also like to be your life partner. Will you marry me, Randi Hollis?"

"Yes!" she shouted, jumping to her feet.

Jasper woofed and then bounced around John as if to say he approved.

John stood and wrapped his arms around Randi, spinning in a circle. He set her down and kissed her, pouring his love into the moment.

When the kiss ended, she said, "I love you, John."

"I love you too. I think I have since you first slid out from under that sink, all wet but full of life."

"We barely know each other."

"We know enough. We'll build on that over time. Maybe wait until the inn's done before we get married?"

"Yes to everything." Laughing, Randi leaned in for another kiss.

EPILOGUE

This was the best day ever. Today, she'd marry John.

The last six months had passed quickly. They'd spent many hours working side-by-side in the inn. At first, they'd expected to take eight to twelve months to reopen the inn. The condition of the property had been better than expected, and her earlier work on the rooms had definitely saved time. When the chef they'd hired was able to start working earlier than expected, they pushed up the open date. And their wedding.

Randi checked her hair in the guest room mirror, tucking in a strand that had escaped the controlled cascade of curls that a hairstylist had coaxed out of her usually straight hair. She stepped back, smiling when she could see her whole dress. She'd asked Bella to design her dress but with trepidation. Randi had seen some of the sophisticated lace dresses that had come out of Wedding Bella. While undeniably beautiful, they were too over-the-top girly for her.

She had a simpler fashion style, and she needed a dress that matched both that style and somehow still fit in with the inn's historic elegance. She thought she'd given Bella an impossible task, but she should have trusted her expertise.

The ruched bodice of the white, strapless satin ball gown joined a full skirt at a pleated waist. Covered buttons ran down the dress from the top to the train Bella had surprised her with. Randi hadn't expected the train, but she loved it. The overall design was simple, elegant, and timeless. Exactly what she'd asked for.

"Hurry up. Hurry up. We need to get you out of here." Michelle handed her the bouquet of pale yellow and white roses. "It's time to go."

"I think you're more nervous than I am, Michelle."

"You don't seem nervous enough."

"There's nothing for me to be concerned about. This is such a good day. I'm marrying my best friend, and the inn looks fabulous."

"Are you sure you're ready to get married? I know you wanted your wedding to take place before the inn officially opened to the public, but you completed the renovation ahead of schedule."

Randi laughed. "I would have married John six months ago. Don't worry. Besides, you got married really quickly."

"Yes, but I'd already dated Sam in high school."

"This Sam is very different from the person you knew then. I mean, he still goes off for weeks at a time and does secret who-knows-what for who-knows-who."

"This is true. But it didn't take me very long to realize that I loved Sam as an adult. Even more than when I thought I'd been in love with him as a teenager." Michelle did a slow pass around Randi. "Everything looks good. And your guests are ready for you outside."

"I just wish Mom and Dad could be here." For the first time, Randi felt a moment of sadness. "When Dad broke his leg two weeks ago, I told them not to try to fly or make a seven-hour drive like that."

"Paige is taking photos today. You'll have great pictures to share with them." Michelle checked the time. "You have to go now. You don't want John to think you're going to stand him up."

Randi confidently walked down the hallway to the inn's staircase. Now polished, the wood gleamed, just as it must have when the inn opened the very first time. Who knows how many feet had come up and down the stairs and the number of weddings that had taken place at the Two Hearts Inn?

They'd thought about changing the inn's name, but Two Hearts Inn not only connected with the town's name but also with them. They had worked as a couple, their two hearts uniting to make this project come to life.

John waited for her at the bottom of the stairs, looking up at her with such love that she felt as if her heart couldn't become any more full.

Randi started down the stairs, holding on to the railing because she had on the requisite high heels with her dress. She'd tried to argue with Bella about hemming her dress for sneakers, but Bella wouldn't hear of it. She did mention ballet flats, but Randi had finally caved and gone with heels. Cassie had later mentioned that Bella had also talked her into high heels, and those had made running away from her wedding more difficult.

Randi had no plans for running away from John.

Each step brought her closer to her groom. Today, he went from fiancé to husband. For a second, nervousness tried to worm its way in, but she pushed it away.

Nervousness only belonged if she was afraid of something, and she wasn't. John had proven himself and his love every minute of the last six months. When she reached the bottom of the stairs, he put his arm out, his elbow crooked for hers to link through.

They'd decided on an unconventional ceremony, with her walking down the aisle with her groom instead of meeting him at the other end. They were in this together, so they'd start out that way. And they didn't have a maid of honor or best man. Just the two of them would stand together for the ceremony.

The lobby was absolutely gorgeous. A variety of yellow and white flowers decorated the railing and lined Randi's path. John had said he didn't care what colors she chose, so that's what she'd gone with. The colors were more springlike than winter, but she enjoyed sunny colors year-round.

Randi knew that when the ceremony itself was over, they'd return inside to the ballroom and dining room. Both rooms were decorated with more flowers and were amazing.

When they neared the back door, he leaned over and whispered, "I love you, soon-to-be Mrs. Morgan."

She giggled. "And I love you too, Mr. soon-to-be Husband."

He grinned at her. And then two people outside—whom Cassie, the wedding planner, must have choreographed—opened the doors so they could exit into what she knew was a stunning garden area. Their friends and family—and probably half the town—were seated, waiting for them.

As the doors opened, the wedding march began, and they walked up the aisle together. A flower girl threw yellow rose petals in their path, a light breeze causing them to billow to the ground.

Earlier in the day, it had been chilly, but by midday, the temperature had warmed up and was pleasant. She'd chosen a long-sleeve wedding gown, though, just in case. She hadn't needed it because the sun was out, making the water sparkle like diamonds.

When they arrived in front of the minister, Randi took her arm away from John's and faced him as they had rehearsed. They reverently spoke the vows they'd written.

As John was saying his vows, she glanced up and noticed that her parents were seated in the front row, her dad's leg stretched out in front of him. She gasped, and John looked over at her with a questioning expression that seemed to ask, *Did you change your mind?*

She whispered, "My parents are here."

He turned to look. "That's great, but, um, is it all right if I go on?"

Randi grinned and said, "Sorry. Please continue."

He promised to love her. To respect her. To support her in all her unusual ideas. To be her rock and best cheerleader.

Randi's smile grew wider. "I, Randi, promise to love you. Honor you. Help you sign books at events. To be there for you when you wake up and when you go to sleep. And to bake chocolate chip cookies when you desperately need them, even though you're a better cook than I am."

He chuckled.

The minister from the church said, "I now pronounce you husband and wife. You may kiss your bride."

And he did just that.

As they walked down the aisle, Randi gave a little wave to her parents, and they both waved back.

John said, "We did it."

She looked over at him. "Got married?"

"Got married in our inn."

"It is good, isn't it?"

"It's awesome. Now you get to have fun being an innkeeper."

"And you get to have fun writing books. With a little time doing maintenance here."

He chuckled. "Anything for you, my love."

Join Cathryn's newsletter to learn when the next book is coming out. And if you've missed it, HOW TO MARRY A

COUNTRY MUSIC STAR is the prequel to the series. Carly is a down-on-her-luck country music star. Jake is the wealthy man who hires her to be his housekeeper. They get married in *Runaway to Romance*. Get the ebook FREE at cathrynbrown.com/marry

ABOUT CATHRYN

Escape into stories that feel like coming home

Cathryn Brown writes clean and cozy romances with a blend of heart, humor, and happily ever afters. Her *Wedding Town Romance* series, set in the fictional small town of Two Hearts, Tennessee, is the perfect escape for readers who love sweet stories with feel-good endings.

She began her writing journey as a journalist and has published hundreds of articles. As Shannon L. Brown, she also writes the *Crime-Solving Cousins Mysteries*, a series for 8–12-year-olds who love fast-paced mysteries with clues, twists, and fun.

Cathryn grew up in Alaska and now lives in Tennessee with her husband and a cat who supervises all writing. She loves baking, hiking, and dreaming up characters who feel like friends.

To explore more of her books, visit CathrynBrown.com.

www.ingramcontent.com/pod-product-compliance
Lightning Source LLC
Chambersburg PA
CBHW031752200726
48289CB00013B/862